A Christmas Wish for Love

MARIAH LYNNE

World Castle Publishing, LLC
Pensacola, Florida
Copyright © 2023 Mariah Lynne
Paperback ISBN: 9798891260528
eBook ISBN: 9798891260535
First Edition World Castle Publishing, LLC, October 2, 2023.
http://www.worldcastlepublishing.com
Licensing Notes
Cover: Cover Designs by Karen
https://www.cover-designs-by-karen.com
Editor: Karen Fuller

CHAPTER ONE

I've always loved everything about Christmas. For as long as I can remember, even without my mom, Christmas was the most magical time of year. Every holiday season, as Dad and I placed the angel on top of our Christmas tree, I admired her beauty and wondered what it would be like to meet a real angel. On the night of my thirteenth birthday, a beautiful spirit surprised me with her visit and changed my dad's and my life forever.

That's how I knew thirteen was my lucky number. My birthday, December 13th, shares the same date as another holiday, The Feast of St. Lucia. Being of Swedish heritage, Mom, knowing she was having a girl, decided that if I was born on that date, my name would be

Lucia, after the saint. I'm proud of my name and spell Luci with an "i" to let people know I'm not a Lucy, short for Lucille. I've always introduced myself as "Luci with an i" to make sure that difference was extra clear.

Sadly, I never met Mom. She died giving birth to me, but Dad honored her wish for my name. Of course, I missed having Mom's love and guidance in my life. I inherited her long blonde curly hair, green eyes, and, as Dad reminded me, her kind nature. From photos, I knew she was beautiful and must have been pretty special for Dad to love her so much. For as long as I can remember, he never dated or talked about meeting someone else, although I could sense how lonely he was without her. I love him more than anyone else in my life and hope someday to change his loneliness, as well as my own, into happiness.

This year, my birthday fell on a Saturday, which was also the first day of our school's holiday vacation. Dad, our local Oleander Island veterinarian, surprised me and prepared a special breakfast of all my favorites. After I finished eating, he shrugged. "Luci, I hate to leave you for part of your birthday, but I just received a text that one of my patients, a Beagle named Princess, fell on a thick branch and will need emergency surgery to remove an abscess in her upper leg. I'll have to go in to help her, but not to worry, our birthday tradition of pizza and pink cupcakes will live on tonight."

I smiled to let Dad know I understood. "It's okay, go help Princess. I would be worried sick if that was Chester." Dad hugged me and left.

Dr. Kyle Mathews, my father, had my adorable three-year-old Labradoodle, Chester, as a patient since Chester was eight weeks old. Chester's former owner had to move off our peaceful island to obtain a better job in town and couldn't take him with her because her new landlord didn't allow pets. She refused to leave Chester in a shelter, and, after telling Dad about her dilemma, he told me he responded, "If you'd let me, I know a young lady, my daughter Luci, who would love Chester to pieces. I'd love to take him home with me."

The woman agreed, sad to lose her one-year-old best friend but happy Chester would have a good home and excellent vet care. Dad was so right. I do love Chester to pieces and knew from our first day together that we were a match made in doggy heaven.

After Chester licked his plate clean, I tidied up the kitchen, all the while looking forward to tonight. Besides my birthday celebration, we decorated our Christmas tree on St. Lucia's Day to honor my mother's family tradition.

Since Chester and I had the entire day free, we decided to visit our next door neighbor, Meta. Meta, in her eighties and from Sweden, has lived alone since her husband died five years ago, and her adult children with families of their own moved off our Gulf Coast Island to find better jobs. Chester and I tried to keep a watchful eye on her. Besides, she was so much fun telling me stories about the old country and loved to cook and bake. Her small island cottage always smelled so delicious.

Chester and I walked over and knocked on her back door. "Hi, Meta, Luci and Chester are here."

I soon heard her sweet, cheerful voice answer. "Yes, my dears, please come in." I liked helping Meta with small household chores whenever I could so she wouldn't hurt herself, but I never expected to find what was waiting for me behind her kitchen door. When I opened it, a swirling white dust storm of flour surrounded me. I waved my hands in the air to move it away, but even so, the dust was so thick I couldn't see anything. Chester rubbed his eyes with his paws and sneezed. It took a few minutes for the dust storm to settle before I saw Meta standing by her kitchen table covered in that same white dust and wearing, from what I could tell, an apron while holding a rolling pin. She made me smile because she looked more like a snowman than a baker. I coughed as some of that fine flour dust filled my throat while Chester sneezed again, trying to get the flour out of his nose.

I think Meta shot me a smile through all that flour. She gushed, "I'm so glad you came. Happy birthday, sweetheart. Your mother would be so proud of the wonderful young lady you've become. Guess what? My youngest son, Andrew, his wife, and my two granddaughters, who are about your age, are arriving tomorrow to spend Christmas with me. There's so much to do. I have to bake holiday cookies, put up the tree, and tidy up the house. I know this mess looks impossible to clean, but this is all just flour I slapped into the air while pounding the dough preparing to roll it out."

Her already white hair appeared whiter, hidden by the soft baking ingredient that also covered her face and clothes. I looked at her and wondered how an eighty-two year old woman, though strong as an ox, could accomplish all that by tomorrow. Meta's always treated me like an adopted granddaughter, so I knew I had to help. She once told me that when she lived in Sweden, she was good friends with my grandparents on Mom's side before they all immigrated to the United States. Chester and I had nothing else planned, and we loved helping Meta. After we finished our chores, we would have treats while she told me about my Swedish heritage and traditions and stories about her as a little girl. I took another look at this human snowman and tried as hard as I could not to laugh. "Meta, we'd like to help. What would you like us to do first?"

Meta paused to think as she shook some of the flour out of her hair and off her apron. "Luci, you're my special angel. Please go into my garage and bring in my tabletop Christmas tree and the three boxes of decorations next to it. Once everything's inside, please decorate my living room."

I laughed. "You're giving me the fun job while you do all the work. We're decorating our tree tonight to honor my mom and St. Lucia's Day."

Meta smiled again. This time, I could tell for sure because her teeth were not as white as her face. "You can't imagine how much I appreciate your help so I can keep baking special treats for the holiday."

"No problem. I'll have Chester wait in the living room while I go into the garage. It's a good thing his former owner sent him for obedience training. Since you're near the sink, please hand me some wet paper towels, and I'll wipe his paws to stop him from dragging flour into your living room. I'll take off my shoes as well before I come back inside."

Chester cooperated as I took each one of his paws and wiped them clean before I took my shoes off. We entered her living room through her unlocked front door. Once Chester settled, I put my sneakers back on outside and went into Meta's amazing garage. It was so organized, I wished my dad's was like that, but he claimed he worked too much and had little time.

I located her small tree covered by a white plastic bag and the boxes labeled lights, manger, and decorations. I carried everything to the front door, removed my sneakers, and took the tree and boxes inside, careful not to break anything.

Once everything was set, I pulled a rawhide chew from my shorts pocket and gave it to Chester so he would stay busy while I helped Meta. I took her pretty blue and white vase from Sweden off the small round side table she always used for her tree and placed it in her china cabinet. Finding a red tabletop lace scarf in the decorations box, I placed it on the table with her tree on top before wrapping the strings of white candle lights in honor of St. Lucia around its branches. I then hung all of her beautiful antique decorations of angels, toy soldiers, and china balls, many in blue and white, just like the china set my grandparents brought over from Sweden.

I draped the fluffy white and silver tinsel garland around the tree before placing her beautiful antique angel with a white silky robe and delicate face on top. I have admired that angel every Christmas for as long as I could remember, and every year, her beauty and long, flowing blonde hair reminded me of photos of Mom. As my thoughts wandered, Meta called. "Luci, please come into the kitchen with Chester and sit with me. I want to show you something."

I walked in expecting to help her take the trash out and sweep up flour, but to my surprise, I found her sitting at her kitchen table. Meta had already swept the flour off the floor, changed her apron, and placed two trays of cookies I couldn't identify behind her on her kitchen counter. The fact that I had never seen those cookies before was amazing because I thought I had tasted every single cookie variety Meta baked.

She placed a red and green pottery plate filled with sugar cookies, a glass of chocolate milk for me, and a box wrapped in silver holiday paper with a big pink bow in the center of the table. I just loved her. Meta knew I loved surprises, and pink was my favorite color. There was a second white box, but not decorated or wrapped.

When the tea kettle whistled, Meta got up and poured herself a cup. She shot me a kind smile. "Luci, I don't know what I'd do without you. I love you like my own grandchild. Today is your birthday, and we must celebrate in style. What kind of adopted grandmother would I be if I forgot your special birthday? Today, you are thirteen and become a young lady."

She placed her cup of tea on the table and sat down. Meta, a strong-willed woman, was someone I would not dream of ignoring, so as instructed, Chester and I both sat next to her. She pushed the holiday dish filled with her traditional Christmas cookies of wreaths, reindeer, and angels, all frosted in white with red and green sprinkles, closer to me. "Please have some. We'll celebrate your birthday and talk."

I chose an angel, thinking about the one on the top of the tree that reminded me of Mom. As I took a quick sip of my chocolate milk and bit into my cookie, Meta continued. "Luci, you were born on a very special day. As a young girl in Sweden, my village celebrated St. Lucia's Day as a very important holiday. December 13th was chosen because many believed the saint died on that date. All of us girls dressed in white robes with a red satin sash around our waists. We were about your age, wore a wreath made of branches on our heads, and all carried a lit candle. One of the young women wore a crown with lit candles. She was our St. Lucia. I remember how excited I was when I was selected to be that girl."

Meta turned and removed an old photo album covered by a clear plastic bag out of a drawer in her counter. She opened it to reveal old black and white photos. Finding a specific page, Meta pointed to a photo of a young lady wearing the crown of lit candles. "That was me. My mother and grandmothers were so proud. They clapped their hands in joy as our processional passed their pew in church. After our service, we served sweet homemade saffron buns to the women of the village. The holiday, also called the Festival of Lights, honored St. Lucia and is in remembrance of her martyrdom. St. Lucia brought food and aid to the Christians hiding in the catacombs of Sicily. She lit her way down to them by wearing the crown of lit candles on her head. That's why we continue to honor her with lit candles." Meta then pushed the silver wrapped box closer to me. "Happy birthday, my wonderful young friend. Go ahead, please open it."

I carefully opened the box, surprised to find a pewter bracelet with a large round charm attached. The etching on the charm was of a beautiful woman wearing the Crown of Lights. I held the bracelet in my hands to admire its details as Meta continued.

"My church presented this bracelet to me on the day I received the crown. I want you to have it. I remember how, before you were born, your wonderful mother insisted that if you were a girl and born on the 13th, your name should be Lucia, just like our saint. I loved your mother very much, and know she's smiling down at us, happy for you to receive this."

Meta put her hand over her heart and looked up at the sky. I didn't know what to say. I loved her like a grandmother and was forever thankful for her motherly influence in my life. I never expected a gift. "Meta, thank you very much. I will treasure this always and think of you every time I wear it."

Meta, tears in her eyes, smiled. "I'm so happy you love it. Let's get to my second box. It's for you to take home and share with your father tonight. Inside are special holiday cookies called Pepparkakor, a St. Lucia's Day tradition. I like to make them in the shape of stars to remember the lights of St. Lucia. Made with ginger, they are delicious to eat, but they also have an important meaning. They are crisp and snap, but you must break them in a very specific way because they are also called Swedish Wishing Cookies."

That aroused my curiosity. I opened the box to find two thin but large cookies shaped like stars. Meta further explained. "You must be extra careful taking them home because many of us Swedes believe these cookies have mystical powers to make your wish happen. Tonight after dinner, you and your dad must each take one out of the box without breaking it. You must place your cookie in the palm of your left hand, close your eyes as tight as you can, and whisper a wish that no one else can hear or understand. Using the thumb on your right hand, press down on the middle of your cookie until it snaps apart. If the cookie breaks into three pieces, your wish will come true, but in order to make this happen, you must then eat the cookie without saying a word."

I loved Meta, and she always charmed me with her stories, but my dad was a man of science, so I was skeptical he would believe any of this. I had to ask. "Meta, that is a beautiful holiday tradition, but have you ever known anyone who had their wish come true? If so, how long did it take?"

Meta squeezed my hand. "Over my

years in my village, many people told me these cookies had granted their wishes. I remember one story in particular, an elder named Stephan. A horse farmer in the mountains above the village, he wanted to sell his farm after his wife died. That Christmas, my mother brought him some of her Wishing Cookies and asked him to break one. He made his wish in silence before he did. His cookie broke into three pieces, so he ate it without saying a word. He didn't have to tell my mother his wish because she could guess. When springtime came, and the snow had partially melted, a few prospective buyers visited the farm, and one purchased it.

"Many others confided that their wish came true the next day, the next week, the next month, but anyone lucky to have the cookie break into three pieces did have their wish come true. I've been told if you believe in the cookie's magic, you will receive a sign to let you know your wish will be granted. I will make a wish tonight for the both of you as well."

I had my scientific father's genes. I

thought maybe the farmer sold because the snow melted, and people could get around easier to look at the property, but I kept that to myself. I glanced at my watch.

"It's four o'clock. Chester and I have to leave to meet Dad. He's bringing home pizza and cupcakes to celebrate. Thank you, Meta, for making my birthday extra special."

I hugged Meta as she told me. "Glad to do it. Remember to have your Wishing Cookies right after dinner and before you decorate the tree. Please make your wish tonight. For some odd reason, I sense the loneliness you both feel in your hearts. Humor this old lady. Who knows? Your wish may come true."

"I will," I answered before Chester and I left for home. I thought about what Meta had just said. Dad and I both miss Mom's love but keep those feelings to ourselves. Chester and I arrived home with enough time to clean up, change, and put a bandana on Chester right before Dad's SUV pulled into our driveway. Maybe Meta's cookie was worth a try? But how will I convince my dad?

CHAPTER TWO

I opened the front door to find Dad balancing two large pizza boxes with a pretty pink bakery box on top. I grabbed the bakery box before it fell, and we took everything straight into the kitchen. Chester followed with his tail wagging and his nose in the air, sniffing the aromas coming from those pizza boxes.

Dad kissed my forehead. "Okay. I'm going to clean up before you tell me all about your day. Sorry I had to leave you alone on your birthday, but I did save that sweet Beagle's leg and life. It was touch and go for a while because of the infection, but she's resting and responding to medication. I didn't want to leave until she was on the mend. That's why I'm later than I thought I would be."

I gave him a big hug and kiss. "Dad, you're the best." He really was. He took the best care of me and always showed an interest in my school work along with my other activities. Besides, Dad taught me a lot about Mom. Every Saturday night since I was old enough to remember, he would go into his closet after dinner and bring out an old shoe box he called his "memory box." It contained memories and photos of Mom from the day she was born to right before my birth. The photos were mixed in with all the greeting cards she gave him over their five years of marriage, but before he removed this special box's lid, he always began the same way.

"Luci, I want you to know that Mom is always with you. She loves you very much and would never abandon her love for you from heaven. I know I tell you this each week, but every night before you and Chester get into bed, wrap your arms around yourself, close your eyes, picture her in your mind, and you will feel her love." The "memory box" became our tradition one as important as the Feast of St. Lucia.

He left but returned soon, wearing a pair of khaki shorts and a T-shirt. He sat at our kitchen table, and I showed him Meta's gift. Dad admired it, telling me. "It's beautiful and shares such a personal memory of hers with you. You said she received it when she wore the Crown of St. Lucia in her church pageant. Meta could have given this bracelet to any one of her six granddaughters but chose to give it to you instead. That must make you feel pretty special."

"It does. It's so lovely and so unique. I love her very much. Meta gave me something else as well. Some thin ginger cookies that are eaten on St. Lucia's Day. She hoped we would have them after dinner."

"I'm sure Meta went to a lot of trouble to bake them, so we'll do just that," Dad said with a smile before he stood and turned the oven on, ready to reheat our dinner. He placed each pie on a large pizza pan and put them into the oven. "Here they go…one large with extra pepperoni for me and one large veggie for you."

I got out plates, silverware, and glasses. I took out a wine glass for Dad. He had a tough day, from the sounds of it. As anticipated, our pizzas were the absolute best! Tony, our local pizza maker, even wrote "Happy Birthday Luci" on the boxes. I was so happy; everyone made me feel so loved today. Once we finished, I brought out Meta's second box and opened it.

"Those stars look and smell delicious," Dad said as he was about to grab one.

"Wait, "I advised, stopping his hand just short of going into the box. "They come with instructions."

"Wow," Dad chuckled. "I never had a cookie that came with instructions."

I gave him a look. "Okay, Mr. Wise Guy, these are baked for St. Lucia's Day and are called Wishing Cookies. You hold the cookie in the palm of your left hand, close your eyes, and make a wish. With your right hand thumb, press on the center of the cookie. If it breaks into three pieces, and you eat the cookie in silence, your wish will be granted."

Dad smiled. "This is some heavy-duty stuff. Do you believe this?"

"I believe in Meta, so I'm going to give it an honest try. Now select your cookie. You have but one chance to do this."

Dad raised his hand like he was in school. I could tell he was having fun with me. "How long, on average, does it take for this magic cookie to work?"

"Meta said she knew of one wish that took months but added your wish could come true the next day. She knew of some that did. Okay. Ready? Choose your weapon."

Dad selected the cookie nearest him. I took the other one. We placed them in our palms and followed Meta's directions when mine broke into three pieces! Dad's crumbled, so I wolfed mine down in silence.

Dad laughed. "Mine was defective. I'd like to know what you wished for because maybe I can make it happen, but I guess that's against the rules." I nodded as he ate his crumbs.

When he finished, he stood to get the pink bakery box. "That was fun but as scientific as a horoscope. Are you ready for your fluffy pink birthday cupcakes?"

I couldn't believe how pretty they were. The frosting had swirls of different shades of pink, and he even bought pink candles. We each had our birthday cupcake, leaving the extra two for tomorrow's dinner and went into the living room to decorate the tree.

He reminded me every year that our tree was bought for Mom and Dad's first Christmas together, and Mom had selected all the decorations. Once the white lights were on and lit to honor Mom and St. Lucia, we hung the beautiful ornaments. As soon as we finished, Dad took something out of his pocket. It was a small box wrapped in Sunday newspaper comics. I opened it to find a silver locket with a photo of Mom on one side and one of me, my newest school photo, on the other. He placed the sterling silver chain around my neck. "Happy birthday, honey. Wear this locket to keep Mom close to your heart like she is to mine."

He became a little teary-eyed as he took a photo of Mom in her wedding gown from his wallet. Twelve years was a long time for us to be without her. I wondered why he never found a woman just to be his friend. Dad was in his late thirties, with light brown hair and brown eyes, rugged looking, and muscular in build. He worked out because some of those pets were pretty hefty. Anyway, I noticed the way women smiled at him. I kissed Dad and thanked him for my unique gift. "This locket is so beautiful I don't know what to say except thank you."

He smiled. "I'm glad you like it. Sorry Luci but I have to go to work again tomorrow morning for just a few hours. I know Sunday's our day, but I have to check on Princess. Don't worry. I'll be back as early as I can."

I gave him a big hug. "Thank you for

such a wonderful night and a wonderful birthday. I'll clean up, so you go get some rest for tomorrow. Princess needs you."

He kissed the top of my head. "Luci, you're the best daughter any Dad could wish for, but you already know I feel that way about you." With that, he turned, yawned, and went into his bedroom. I cleaned up all the wrappings, birthday paper plates, and pink plastic silverware. Chester stayed by my side. Finished, we went to my room.

I kissed the photo of Mom in my new locket. I missed her all the time but, especially after I visited my friends' homes. Their moms treated me with extra kindness and told me they would always be there to listen to my feelings. I knew they weren't trying to make me sad, but saying that made me realize how much I missed not having Mom in my life. I'd love to have her back, but since that was impossible, I did that hug for her every night before Chester and I went to bed. I wrapped my arms around myself, ready to send Mom my love. Chester and I were so beat we fell asleep as soon as our heads hit the pillows, but I woke up suddenly when I heard Chester utter a low growl.

A surreal white light filled my room, making everything look hazy. Chester looked at it and growled again. The hair on the nape of his neck stood straight up as his eyes focused on the foot of my bed. When I looked there, my eyes opened so wide I could feel my eyelashes touch my eyebrows because, as the haze cleared, the most beautiful woman I had ever seen in my life with long blonde curly hair like mine and green sparkling eyes stood by the foot of my bed staring back at me. She looked like the photo of Mom in my locket, but I knew it couldn't be her. Wearing a loose-fitting white robe with a garland of ivy around her waist, she had a wreath of ivy in her hair.

I was so surprised. All I could say was, "Who are you? You're so beautiful you're either a dream or a spirit sent by my Wishing Cookie to make my wish come true."

The beautiful woman touched Chester's

head. He became calm as his growl turned into a whimper. She then reached for my hand. "Luci, I'm not a dream. I'm the spirit of your mother. I came because I heard your wish to Meta's cookie."

My jaw dropped so fast it almost hit the bed. "You mean like a ghost or a fairy godmother?"

The spirit shot me a tender smile. "Neither, though if I had a choice, I'd rather be your fairy godmother. As her spirit, I'm the essence of her love. Please don't be afraid. I love you and your father more than you can imagine."

I had to pinch myself to see if I was really awake. Surprised that I was, I listened as she continued. "I've kept my eyes on you both every day since I left and know you're doing fine physically, but sense a silent loneliness in your hearts you both endure and realize you need a woman's touch, a motherly influence, and a loving companion for Dad. I heard you when you wished for that. Your whispers brought me here to help."

I grabbed onto my locket as tight as I could and moved up further away from her on the bed, not knowing how she felt about my wish. I hoped she wasn't upset and this entire episode was just a sugar high from my birthday cupcake and Meta's cookie, but she continued.

"I understand you long for a woman's touch in your life, not because you don't love or miss me but because Dad is lonely and often sad. I know you need a mother figure as well. You're doing a wonderful job of taking care of Dad, but he needs more in his life, and so do you. I see how sad you get after you visit your friends and how Dad stares at our wedding photo. You wonder if your wish angers me. I love you and Dad and only want the best for both of you, so the answer is 'no.'"

She walked around the side of my bed and sat. Her hand caressed my face. "Luci, you will meet someone very soon who will fill that void. Please keep your eyes, ears, and heart open to welcome her. She will make you as happy as those chocolate kisses wrapped in silver foil I loved to eat made me. I must leave you, but remember, as Dad tells you, I'm always with you. You may even find me in different forms of nature because I'm always watching over you.

"By the way, keep sending those nightly hugs. They are so wonderful, but please promise not to tell anyone about my visit."

Still in shock, I could only respond with a nod before she blew me a kiss and vanished into the night, along with the bright white haze.

I knew Chester saw her as well. He was on his back, wagging his tail and panting with his tongue out like he was in love. Maybe it wasn't the cupcake or a dream? Maybe she did come because of my wish? I sure hope so, but after seeing her, how will I ever fall back to sleep?

CHAPTER THREE

That next morning, another bright light startled me awake. I shot up in bed only to have my hopes of seeing Mom again shut down when I realized the light was morning sun pouring in through my bedside window. That amazing vision of Mom's beautiful spirit still lingered in my mind as I looked over at Chester, who slept as sound as a baby. I sure wished he spoke human so we could compare notes.

I looked around my room to make sure we were alone. Everything seemed normal, so I got up, got dressed, and kissed Chester. He stirred but didn't get up, so I went into the kitchen to make Dad breakfast before he left for the clinic. I knew better than to tell him about the visit from Mom's spirit, no matter how wonderful it was. Besides, I promised not to and prided myself in keeping my word.

Dad liked to make his own coffee, so I toasted a blueberry muffin with butter and gave him a banana. He looked at me and grinned. "I won't be long, sweetie. You and Chester do something fun this morning while I'm gone. We'll continue our celebration later this afternoon. By the way, your locket looks beautiful on you."

With that, he kissed me and left for the clinic. After sleepyhead Chester and I finished our breakfasts, we decided to go for a walk. We walked by Meta's house. There was a second car in her driveway, probably that of her relatives, so we decided to keep going. Suddenly, a beautiful red cardinal flew out from one of Meta's crimson hibiscus bushes and hovered back and forth right in front of us.

The cardinal continued to fly ahead of us, swerving back and forth, when all of a sudden, he made a sharp turn into a driveway three houses down from Meta's. Curious, Chester and I followed only to see that the "For Sale" sign that had been there forever read "Sold," and moving boxes filled the driveway. Our former neighbors, the Browns, must have sold their house and moved. Since I was curious to the point of getting myself into trouble, Chester and I made a beeline into that driveway. There was a bright royal blue SUV in the yard with its trunk open and loaded with more boxes. The cardinal flew and perched on the nearest bush facing the SUV.

Eager to learn more, we walked around the car just as we heard someone come out the front door. I looked over to see a beautiful woman with short, dark, curly hair and large brown eyes. She smiled when she saw us. "Hi. May I help you?"

I blushed, embarrassed she found me snooping and responded with the first thing that came to mind. "Welcome to our neighborhood. I'm Luci with an 'i', and this handsome young man is Chester. We love helping our neighbors, so if we can assist you in any way, please let us know. I go to The Beach School and am on Christmas break, so I have the next two weeks off. From what I can see, you have a lot of stuff to unpack. Are your kids here to help?"

That got a chuckle out of her. "No kids, no husband. It's just me moving in. I do have a cat, Cosmic Cosmo, a Tabby, who's boarding at the island veterinary clinic until I get myself organized. Luci, with an 'i', do you help your other neighbors?"

"Mostly my next door neighbor Meta because she's elderly and so kind to me. I've known her my whole life. That's so great your Cosmic Cosmo's at the vet because the island vet is my dad, and he takes the best care of all his patients and borders. He went to work on my birthday to help a Beagle who had an abscess. Will you be working on the island?"

"My, you sure do ask a lot of questions. When you grow up, you should be a news reporter. Yes, in a little less than two weeks, I start a new position as head librarian at the Beach Library."

Her answer got me excited. "That's so cool because you'll be seeing a lot of us once school is back in session. Chester is a certified reading dog, and we go every other Saturday so the first and second graders can read to him. Since I told you my name, what's yours?"

"I'm Sage Domano. Nice to meet you, Luci, with an 'i'. That's quite a unique name."

I shuffled my feet. "I know. Everyone tells me that. I was born on St. Lucia's Day, so my full name is Lucia, after the saint and not Lucy from Lucille. I'm very fussy about being called the right Luci."

Sage shot me a smile. "I can tell. Since yesterday was St. Lucia's Day, happy birthday." I watched Sage look at all the boxes in the driveway and the back of her SUV. "You know there are more unpacked boxes in the house that I've already carried in. My movers are bringing the furniture Tuesday, so the more of these I get unpacked, the better I'll be. I guess I could use help, but only with these two conditions. One is that you give your mother my business card and have her check up on me before you come back with a note of approval. I taught junior high school English before becoming a librarian, and I know all about stranger danger. I told my classes not to talk to strangers like you're doing with me and for sure not to go anywhere alone with them, especially into any building.

"Two, I insist on paying you. Please ask her if minimum wage is okay and tell her you won't be doing any heavy lifting, only unwrapping and unpacking."

"I understand," I said as I took her business card that had all of her social media sites printed on it. I didn't want to burst her bubble. I didn't want a job. I just loved helping people. I paused. "But I'll have to ask my dad. Mom died when I was born."

Sage gave me a caring glance and paused as if she didn't know what to say. "Luci, I'm so sorry, honey. I didn't know. I lost someone very dear to me as well, so I know how painful that loss can be in your heart. Please ask your dad if he's not too busy keeping my little terror Cosmic Cosmo in line."

Her last statement made me laugh. "I will. If he says 'yes,' what time would you like Chester and me to come tomorrow?"

"Hmmm. I'm not a good early morning person. Need that coffee first thing. How about nine-thirty?" Sage responded.

"Sounds good to me. If I can't come, I'll call the phone number on your card."

"Great. Hope I see you both tomorrow." She walked over and gave Chester a big hug. "Can't help it, he's so sweet." She waved and went back into her house.

Chester and I headed for home with that pretty red cardinal following us all the way back. My mind was filled with questions. Sage was single, looked about Dad's age, must be smart to be head librarian, and loved pets. Best of all, besides being very pretty, she was looking out for me. Could Meta's cookie be working, and did my mom's spirit guide me to her? Her spirit did say it would happen soon and to keep my eyes and heart open, while Meta said her cookie could work the next day. It didn't matter which one led me to Sage. It's too much for a young girl like me to figure out. I can't let my imagination get the better of me.

I looked over to see that pesky cardinal flying close enough to land on my shoulder as he bobbed back and forth. It was eleven a.m., and Meta's house was next. I stopped by to greet her family and knocked on her front door. When Meta opened it, that cardinal scurried right past her and landed on the Hibiscus bush next to her front door. He chirped as loud as he could. Of course, Meta noticed him right away. She put her finger over her mouth to let me know to be quiet. "Luci, is this bird following you?"

I nodded. "I don't know why. He's been doing that all morning, and I don't have any birdseed on me."

Meta looked pleasantly surprised. "Before we go inside to see my family, I want to tell you something about the cardinal. Many believe seeing a red cardinal is a sign from a loved one who has passed away. The cardinal is believed to be a spiritual guide with a special message that signals a new chapter in your life. I'm so excited to see this young man and hope he may have something to do with our Wishing Cookie."

Meta squeezed my cheeks and smiled. "Come, let's see my family. Not a word about what I just told you. They don't believe in such things like I do." I followed Meta inside to hugs and kisses, holiday treats with hot chocolate, and for being thankful for Meta's love.

CHAPTER FOUR

Dad arrived home about an hour after Chester and I did. He smiled and kissed my forehead. "I'm going to shower and change so you can tell me all about your day. By the way, Princess is resting and on the mend. She should be able to go home Tuesday."

Excited, I couldn't wait to tell him about my day and ask for that note for Sage. He returned in shorts and a T, and Chester and I sat with him in our small but cozy living room.

I gushed. "I did do something special today. Remember the Browns' house? Someone bought it, and I met our new neighbor." I took Sage's business card out of my pocket. "Her name is Sage, and she moved here to be our island's new head librarian. After seeing how many moving boxes she had, I asked if she could use some help unpacking. She said she could, but before I could help, she wanted you to check up on her and, if it's okay, bring her a note before I start. She said to give you her card and even offered to pay me. She seemed really nice, and you know how much I love to help people."

I handed Dad her business card and added. "Oh, and you're taking care of her cat, Cosmic Cosmo, until she gets settled."

"Cosmic Cosmo? Huh. He's quite a handful." Dad said with a wink. "I'll call someone on the library board first thing in the morning and check up on her. If everything's okay, I'll drive you there and meet her in person since she's our new neighbor."

Sounded excellent to me. I again wondered if his meeting Sage had anything to do with Mom's visit or my Wishing Cookie or if it was just his way of being careful. Guess I'll have to wait until tomorrow morning to find out. I knew Dad was tired, so I heated up our pizza for an early dinner, and we enjoyed another birthday celebration with candles and cupcakes. Hope all that sugar doesn't make me have another vision, no matter how wonderful it was to meet my mom. Chester and I went to my room only to hear loud fluttering and chirping outside my window. That pesky cardinal was sitting on my windowsill, trying to get in. Why won't he leave me alone?

I woke up Monday morning to find no more fluttering, no more chirping, and no more flying. That cardinal left, but I did hear Dad grinding coffee beans and making coffee. I got dressed and was ready to make him breakfast, but I waited in the hall outside the kitchen because I overheard him make a phone call to Gus, a member of the library board. "Hey, Gus. This is Dr. Mathews. How's Spot doing? Great. Happy to hear that. Anyway, I wanted to touch base with you. You know my daughter Luci and her dog Chester since they participate in the reading dog program. Thanks for asking. They're both fine. I needed to know if a Sage Domano will be our head librarian in two weeks. Yes, she will. Did you or the board find anything of concern in her past? No nothing. The reason for all these questions is that Ms. Domano is our newest neighbor, and Luci wants to help her unpack. Ms. Domano insisted I check her references first. All good, you say. Former junior high school teacher. Wonderful. Thanks for your time. I appreciate it."

I walked in as soon as he hung up. Sleepy head Chester followed. "Hi, Dad, love you. How does cinnamon raisin toast with cream cheese sound?"

He smiled. "Sounds great, you know I appreciate everything you do. By the way, I finished checking Ms. Domano's references, and she's good to go. I'm glad you're dressed because as soon as we finish breakfast, I am going to drive you and Chester over there so I can meet her in person and see what she's like before you start to help her."

We finished our two orders of cinnamon

raisin toast with cream cheese while Chester did the same to his salmon and beef dogfood. Dad locked the house, and off we went. I looked at my watch; oh no, it was only eight-thirty.

"Dad, Sage said she wasn't an early bird and asked me to come at nine-thirty. We're an hour early."

"Can't help it, honey. I have to go to the clinic. I'm sure she'll be fine with this. You seem to like her, and she asked me to check her references, so she must like you too. Besides, this way, I can give her my approval in person."

We drove four houses down. Dad parked behind her SUV, and the three of us walked to her front door and rang the bell. We soon heard "Coming."

When Sage opened the door, she had on a pale pink chenille robe. Her short, dark, curly hair was a mess, and she wore no make-up. Even so, in the morning sunlight, she looked as beautiful as ever. Her olive complexion glowed. I looked at Dad. By the expression on his face, I think he thought the same thing.

She stepped outside and offered her hand to shake. As soon as their eyes met, he started to introduce himself but became tongue-tied. I've never ever seen him like this before.

He took a deep breath. "Excuse the interruption, Ms. Domano. I'm Dr. Mathews, Luci's Dad. I wanted to meet you before she helps you unpack."

Sage smiled an irresistible smile. "I'm glad you did. Please excuse my appearance. I didn't expect anyone this early. May I offer you a cup of coffee? Please come in. I just ground some beans."

Dad's awkward smile remained on his face. "Thank you, perhaps another time. I have to go into the clinic to make sure your Cosmic Cosmo's behaving."

They both laughed. The only funny thing to me was I felt like I wasn't even there. I kicked Dad's ankle. He looked at his watch.

"Okay, Luci, I can tell you're in good hands. Oh, Ms. Domano, Luci enjoys assisting neighbors. She does it because she loves to help and doesn't expect to get paid. If you'd like, you can donate to our small island no-kill animal shelter instead."

Sage nodded. "Please call me Sage, and I'd be happy to do that."

Once Dad left for work, Chester and I followed Sage inside. She smiled. "Please give me a minute, Luci, so I can make myself presentable. I'll be right back. That's nice of your father to drive you here and shows he really cares about your well-being. Make yourself comfortable, which I know is hard to do with only folding chairs and TV tables."

Chester and I walked into her living room, which opened into a small dining area. Sage had already moved the rest of the boxes from her car and driveway inside. Each box was marked with the room and contents on the top, like books for bookcase, items for living room, dining room dishes, Christmas decorations, etc. She sure thought like a librarian cataloging everything. I saw a folding chair in the living room and sat down. Chester lay by my feet.

The TV table next to me had a pretty glass candy dish with a lid. I knew it was too early for sweets, but I looked inside anyway. What's this? Chocolate kisses wrapped in silver foil? Sage walked in on my snooping just as I continued to stare at those chocolate kisses. She chuckled. "A bit early for sweets, but please enjoy some later. Those chocolate kisses are my absolute favorite."

My hands shook a little after that statement, so I carefully closed the lid, adding, "Can't lie. I was being nosey. I'm not allowed to eat candy in the morning, no matter how tempting. I met someone the other night who loved those kisses as well."

Sage smiled. "No worries. Ready to get to work? I moved the boxes into the rooms where the contents belonged. Please do not lift any of them. Just unwrap, dust, and put away what you can. What you can't, I'll push out of the way of the movers."

I nodded and started with the easiest: the boxes of books. Sage's house had a built-in bookcase that went halfway up her living room wall, so I unpacked those boxes first. Wow! She had each box numbered by type. She must want me to put them away that way. She left a roll of paper towels, so I dusted the books as I unpacked them. I started with the top shelf and followed the numbers on the boxes until they were all put away. The next box nearest the bookcases was marked photos. I opened the box to find framed photos, which, according to her note taped to that box, were to go on top of the bookcase.

I saw a cute one of her with Cosmic Cosmo, a very chunky cat, one of her college graduation photo, and a few I assumed were family photos. I came across one I couldn't place. It was of a handsome soldier in camouflage. He had ruddy cheeks, big blue eyes, a very nice smile, and light brown hair. As I stared at it, Sage came back into the living room. "Wow. You put all those books away and even started on the photos. Thank you." Holding that soldier's photo, I looked up at her.

Sage took a deep breath. "I see you've met Brandon. Like I said yesterday, I also know the pain of losing someone I loved. He was the love of my life, and my love for him is still strong. That photo was taken during what was supposed to be his last tour in Afghanistan."

Sage's eyes swelled with tears. "After he finished that tour, we planned to be married, but that wasn't meant to be. He was killed when the caravan he was in suffered a sneak attack. I miss him every day, but I'm sure you know that feeling all too well. Say, why don't we talk about something happy, take a break, and each enjoy two of my chocolate kisses. You'd be surprised at how much energy they give you."

I looked into her eyes. They had an all too familiar sad expression like Dad's. I changed the subject. "Cosmic Cosmo sounds like quite the handful. I'm sure Dad will tell us funny stories about him. Why did you name him that?"

Sage handed me two kisses. "Because he

chases his tail around and around so fast one day he'll spin himself into orbit."

I laughed at that before I tasted one chocolate kiss. They were so good I ate the second right away and could see why Mom loved them so much.

"Okay, Luci, with an 'i', time to go back to work. When you finish the photos, please go into the dining room. I lucked out. The former owner had glass front cabinets built in with countertops. I didn't have any china cabinets because I don't have china, only what I call my fancy dishes, so you can unpack all the boxes in the dining room and put the stuff away. I put sticky notes to indicate what goes where. My Holly and Ivy Christmas dishes are in there as well."

Her notes made that job so easy. I stayed until three-thirty, just enough time to finish the dining room. She understood. "Luci, I know you have to leave to make dinner for your dad. I want you to know how much I appreciate your help." Sage came over and gave both of us a big hug. "Thank you. You both are very special to help me."

Chester and I walked home in silence, all the while my mind spinning with more what-ifs. Could those chocolate kisses be a sign like Mom said from my Wishing Cookie or maybe from Mom herself? I wished I could figure this entire thing out.

Once home, I took a quick shower and started to prepare baked chicken with an easy recipe from my kid's cookbook. I added carrots and potatoes and covered it.

Lucky I started dinner late because Dad came home a little later than I expected. He was all smiles. "Hey, sweetie, I stopped by Sage's to give you a ride home, but you had already left. She said her furniture will arrive tomorrow late morning, and you're going over to help again. She seems very nice and gave me a check for a one hundred dollar donation to the shelter. You must be either doing a bang-up job, or she's an animal lover. Guess she'd have to be one to put up with Cosmic Cosmo." Dad laughed. "That cat's quite a handful. My assistants are having a heck of a time with him. Anyway, she said she wanted to do something nice for you for helping her and for me for allowing you to do so. She invited us over for dinner Thursday night at six-thirty. I thought that seemed too soon considering she just moved in, but she said not to worry, so I accepted if that's okay with you."

If my jaw had dropped any lower, it would have hit the floor. He never accepted invitations from single women he didn't know or even did know, for that matter. I closed my mouth. "That sounds great, Dad. Is Chester invited?"

"He sure is. Anyway, I'm starved. Let me go clean up." He left and returned shortly. As we both enjoyed our chicken dinner, he asked, "Do you think Sage would like some flowers and a nice wine?"

Wow! What is going on here?

CHAPTER FIVE

Dad drove me to Sage's early again this morning. Chester and I could have walked, but for some reason, he must have wanted to see her again. Sage surprised me as well. When she opened her front door, I noticed she was dressed in jean shorts and a red top like she expected us that early. I watched as Dad and Sage gazed into each other's eyes like teenagers on a date. They were so cute. I wondered if something magical was really happening.

Even with all the unpacking we had left to do, Sage made everything fun for us. We sang Christmas carols. She told me funny stories about her as a little girl over the holidays, like the year she was the angel in her church's nativity scene. "I forgot to put on my white satin angel shoes; instead, I kept on my dirty sneakers. My mother was so embarrassed when some audience members noticed them. She told me later she overheard them whisper, "Look at how adorable she is," but by her stern look, I'm sure Mom didn't think so."

I loved spending time with Sage but knew we had to get our work done because her furniture delivery was on its way. Starting in the kitchen, I put away pots and pans, everyday dishes, and silverware because, like yesterday, her notes told me where to store everything. The movers arrived late morning, right on time, and placed the furniture in the rooms as she instructed. Once they left, Sage took a deep breath. "Glad that's done. Let's take a short break for some of my favorite chocolate kisses before we begin to unpack again."

The house looked so pretty. Sage sighed. "Luci, I'm lucky the former owners painted the inside of the house before they decided to sell it. I love the soft peach color in the living room and dining room."

We each had two kisses like before, as Sage advised me. "I'll take care of my bedroom, office, and guest bathroom. You know you and your dad are coming to dinner Thursday night, so I hoped you would help me get ready and decorate the house for Christmas. I asked the movers to place the tree in front of the window and the boxes of ornaments next to it."

I laughed. "I'd love to do that! I just decorated Meta's house."

"You sure are everyone's Christmas elf," Sage chuckled. The very second she finished that comment, an SUV pulled into her driveway. Chester barked while I asked. "Why is Dad here? It's only one-thirty, and I go home at three."

There was a knock on her front door. When Sage opened it, she greeted Dad with a sweet smile. "Hi Kyle, this is a nice surprise." He winked at me and gave her the biggest smile I'd seen on his face in years. He carried in a brown grocery bag and placed it on her kitchen table since, by now, she had one. "There is a tuna sub cut in half, two large chocolate chip cookies, and two root beers. I hope you like root beer, Sage. It's my Luci's favorite."

Sage appeared surprised and happy. "This is very kind of you. I do like root beer. It's my favorite as well."

Dad, still in his scrubs, walked over and kissed the top of my head. "I have to leave and get back to the clinic. See you later, Luci. Sage, we're both looking forward to Thursday night."

Sage then walked Dad to the front door and outside to his car. I could see them through the front windows. They lingered for a short while before he got in. It was like their eyes did not want to let go of the others.

Dad left as quickly as he came. Sage and I shared lunch before we went back to work. Kitchen finished, I decided to open the tree branches and decorate her tree. It was a tall artificial blue spruce. The movers had already positioned the tree behind her couch and in front of her living room window so the lights could be seen outside at night. Sage peeked in and gave me a thumbs up, so I opened the boxes of decorations and put on her blue lights first before hanging her ornaments. She collected snowmen, and they all looked so cute under the blue lights. I added her silver garland and found her tree topper. OMG! It was another angel, but this one had dark brown hair and eyes and wore a pale blue silky robe. Kind of looked like Sage. I put the timer on the lights like I do at our house and lit the tree. It looked so pretty. Sage came in and gushed. "You did an amazing job. Everything's perfect. My mother gave me that angel. She said it reminded her of me."

I looked at my watch. "Better run. Dad should be home soon, and Chester needs his dinner. See you tomorrow night. Come on, Chester, let's go."

Just as we started to leave Sage's, Dad pulled up near her driveway. He rolled down his window. "Hey, you two need a lift?" He looked happy as he waved to Sage, who was standing in her front doorway. Chester and I hopped in, and we all started for home. All the way, Dad asked what seemed like a million questions about how my day at Sage's went, starting with, "Did Sage want to know any more about me?"

CHAPTER SIX

I couldn't wait. Dinner at Sage's tonight. She said she loved to cook Italian. The only Italian food I've ever had was pizza and spaghetti with sauce from a jar. I dressed up for the occasion, choosing a red and white dress. I put on my new locket and bracelet and tied sparkly red and green Christmas ribbons to Chester's collar. Dad knocked. "Ready?"

When I opened my bedroom door, Dad looked extra handsome in a long-sleeve light blue dress shirt and tan dress pants. He must have thought tonight was pretty special, too. He never gets that dressed up unless it's for church or an island wedding. When I complimented him on his choice of clothes, all he could say was, "I wanted to look respectful for your new friend."

Respectful? Are you kidding me? He looked down-right great!

As the three of us pulled into her driveway, I noticed Sage had the tiny red and green lights around the wreath on her front door lit. Dad carried a large pot of red and pink poinsettias and a bottle of wine while I held onto Chester's leash.

She must have heard our car pull up because she opened the door to greet us. Sage looked so pretty wearing a deep red blouse, a red and black skirt, and a Christmas apron with snowmen on it. Dad smiled. "Hi, Sage. We've been looking forward to tonight since you invited us." He held up the poinsettias and handed her the bottle of wine as we made our way inside. "Where would you like me to put these?"

Sage gushed. "I thought I told you not to bring anything. This is my treat, but thank you so much. The poinsettias are so beautiful in red and pink. They'll be lovely next to my tree. And the wine, Sangiovese, is perfect for an Italian dinner. You both look wonderful, and Chester's so cute with his holiday ribbons."

We followed her to the living room. I noticed she had put up more decorations after I left yesterday; green and gold garlands framed her bookcases, wide red candles in wooden holders were lit on her coffee table alongside a candy dish shaped like a snowman's face and filled with hard ribbon candy. Her tree was lit, and the lights in her living room dimmed.

When I peeked into the dining room, it looked like Mrs. Claus paid her a visit to help. Sage set the table with a holly and ivy patterned tablecloth, matching dishes, candle sticks with red candles, and green water and wine goblets. Sage gushed. "I'm so happy you could come. I'm alone this holiday season, so to have new friends is a gift. Please sit down and make yourself comfortable. Luci, the tree looks beautiful. Thanks for helping me decorate."

She excused herself to go into the kitchen only to return with a cheeseboard, crackers, and a dip. "I love this dip. It's a ham and scallion dip in a cream cheese base. Please help yourselves, but remember I cooked my heart out today, so save some room."

Dad laughed. "I didn't eat all day in anticipation, so there's plenty of room in there." He rubbed his stomach. "Chester's the only full one here."

Sage then asked. "May I get you something to drink to go with these appetizers? I know Luci likes root beer, Kyle wine, or scotch, or something else?"

"Scotch would be great, but only a little bit on ice since I have to drive." That's my dad, always cautious and reserved. That's why I was so surprised to see him this happy at Sage's.

Sage enjoyed a glass of wine. Dad sipped his scotch while I drank my root beer. We all munched on her dip and cheeses. They talked non-stop about their pasts, their likes, their jobs, their hopes. So much so I felt like I was on their first date. Sage looked at her watch. "Dinner's ready. Please look for your place card and sit down." Wow, place cards. She went all out. Dad and I followed Sage's directions. My place card had a reindeer. Dad's an elf. Sage popped out of the kitchen with a large tray filled with sliced meats, vegetables, and small pieces of cheese made into balls. She brought out a basket of sliced thin bread and serving forks. "First course. Antipasto. Dig in."

Say no more we did. As we enjoyed our antipasto, Sage told us a little about herself. "I grew up in an Italian-American neighborhood. My grandparents came from a small village outside of Naples. They were warm, giving, and loved to cook. I made for you tonight my Nona's pasta recipe my mom makes at Christmas. Not to worry, we had turkey with it as well. Since I'll be alone this year, I loved the idea of sharing this dish with my two new friends."

She left the table again only to bring out a platter of meatballs. "May I help you?" Dad asked as Sage nodded.

"No, this is my pleasure. Luci helped

me so much. I wanted to do something special for you both." She then brought out a deep casserole dish filled with small round pasta in a different-looking sauce. As she put the casserole dish on the table, she told us about it. "This marinara sauce is made with ricotta cheese, and parmesan whisked into it. The pasta is small, so it absorbs all the cheese flavors. Mom made the pasta fresh and rolled it with her fingers to get that shape. I can't lie. I special ordered some at the Italian deli and market off the island where they make all kinds of fresh pasta."

Dad took a deep breath. "Boy, does that smell delicious."

Sage smiled. "May I serve you?" I nodded right away. This was too special to pass up. She scooped out two serving spoons filled with the pasta and added a meatball. Wow, did that ever look great.

I waited for Dad to be served and for Sage to serve herself before I dug in. Once we started eating, no one uttered a single word.

Her dinner was that good. Sage broke the silence, "Kyle, thank you again for the wine. It's the perfect choice," she said as she refilled their wine glasses.

After we all had seconds and cleaned our plates, Dad sighed. "This holiday meal was amazing. You said you have this every Christmas?"

Sage nodded. "It's my Italian family's tradition. My Grandma brought the recipe over with her from Naples, Italy."

I interjected. "That was the best Italian food I've ever had in my entire life."

Sage grinned. "I'm so happy to hear that." As she stood to take the casserole dish and platter of meatballs into the kitchen, she added. "Thank you, Luci, I'm glad you enjoyed it." Chester whimpered under the table. I was sure hoping someone would drop a morsel of meatball before that platter left the dining room. We all laughed at Chester's antics as Dad helped Sage clear the table.

When they returned and were seated,

Dad surprised me by starting the conversation. "Sage, Luci and I are members of the island's marine science center. This coming Saturday night is their annual holiday fundraiser. A popular island restaurant near the fishing docks cooks locally caught fish and chips, followed by a silent auction. I donate a $100 gift certificate for pet care. I bought ten dinner tickets today for us and my staff. I know this is short notice, but we'd love to have you join us."

Sage giggled. "You don't have to ask me twice. I'll be there with bells on. I love silent auctions, especially for a good cause. What time does it start?"

"The auction starts at seven, and people can bid for two hours before they close the bids. They use a separate room to display the donations alongside their bidding sheets. If we get there by five-thirty, we can eat first and listen to a local band before we shop 'til we drop, so we'll have to leave at four-thirty because of the island's holiday traffic."

"Four-thirty it is. Should I meet you at the auction or at your house? I always manage to buy things at these events. I'm excited! What fun!"

Dad responded. "We'll be happy to pick you up."

Sage nodded. "Thank you. I appreciate that since I'm not sure about the marine science center's location. Now, who's ready for dessert?" I raised my hand at once. She didn't have to ask me twice. That made Dad and Sage smile. She left us to return with a tray of goodies. Cannoli, she said she purchased, lemon and orange cookies she said baked using another family recipe, and a large biscuit for Chester. Sage thought of everything. "Luci, more root beer?" I shook my head 'yes'. "Kyle coffee? I already made some, so it's no trouble."

He responded. "Yes, please, black."

We finished our desserts before I asked. "May I help with the dishes?" Sage shook her head. "No, Luci, this evening was my pleasure. I'm so glad you both came and enjoyed dinner.

I made a ton of pasta, as you saw from the size of my casserole dish. May I send some home with you? The leftovers are terrific."

Dad was about to say "no," but I was quicker. "Yes, please."

Sage went into the kitchen and returned with an aluminum foil pan covered with a sheet of foil and placed it on the table. "I added extra sauce to the pasta and meatballs. Please enjoy it tomorrow night. I'm so excited about Saturday night. This will be my first beach event."

Dad moved his hand to touch hers. "We're glad you can come. Six a.m. comes early, so I guess we should think about leaving." Dad picked up the foil pan as Chester and I got up to leave. Sage followed us to our car.

He placed the food on the front seat of his car while we jumped into the back seat. Turning to Sage, he said. "This was an amazing dinner and evening. Thank you." Their eyes lingered in one another's for quite a few minutes before she stepped back and waved. "See you Saturday at four-thirty."

Dad headed the SUV for home. He hummed Christmas carols all the way back. Sure sounded like he was looking forward to Saturday night, maybe even more than I was.

CHAPTER SEVEN

So much has happened between Thursday night's dinner at Sage's and the Saturday night auction and fish fry. We enjoyed the dinner Sage sent home with us. It was as yummy as it was last night. When we finished, Dad relayed what happened today when Sage picked up Cosmic Cosmo from boarding. "My staff was happy to see Cosmic Cosmo leave. He was so rambunctious and fussy. I guess he's a one woman cat because Cosmic Cosmo screeched at the top of his lungs when he saw Sage. He calmed down as soon as Sage put him in his kennel. I helped her carry the kennel to her car. All the way, that crazy cat put his paws through the wire kennel door, trying to get at me."

"Did he scratch you?" I asked, concerned.

"No honey, I wore gloves," Dad replied with a smile, but I realized he had to put himself in danger, no matter how small, to help his patients.

I cleaned up the dishes and was just about to go into the living room and watch TV with Dad when the phone rang. I answered right away, hoping Dad didn't have an emergency. "Hello, this is Luci with an 'i.'"

A familiar voice responded. "Luci, this is Sage. Cosmic Cosmo pawed the lock on his kennel door open and got loose. My back screen door was ajar enough for him to escape. He's on the run, and I can't find him. Would you help me? I'm afraid he might get hurt. It might be a good idea to leave Chester home."

What else could I say? I knew how much that crazy cat meant to her. "Sure, I'll be right there." I hung up just as Dad came back into the kitchen.

Curious, he asked. "Who was that?"

I sighed. "It was Sage, Dad. Cosmic

Cosmo's loose and on the run, and she needs help catching him. She's afraid he might get hurt."

Dad laughed. "I told you that cosmic cat was a handful. I'd be more concerned he'd scratch or hurt anyone who tried to get near him. Okay. Let's go help. I leave a pair of work gloves in the car." Dad then grabbed his keys, a flashlight, and went to the front door. When he opened the door, I heard him say. "Easy, boy, I'm not going to hurt you." I peeked to see who was there, and to my surprise, there sat Cosmic Cosmo. He meowed as Dad instructed. "Luci, quick, grab my extra pair of work gloves and bring them to me as soon as possible. Keep Chester away from the door."

I dashed to find his work gloves and handed them to him before I escorted Chester to my room and closed the door. Dad kept our front door partially closed to prevent Cosmic Cosmo from sneaking inside. He spoke in a calm, soft voice, not to scare off our guest. "Well, look here. It's Cosmic Cosmo. Guess I made a good impression on you. Would you like to come inside? Stand back, Luci. I'm going to grab him. Once I do, call Sage."

I couldn't believe what was happening. Dad bent over to pick up Cosmic Cosmo, and that crazy cat let him, purring like a kitten before snuggling into Dad's chest. I always knew my dad had a way with animals, but this was unbelievable. Maybe he pawed at Dad so he would take him back. Since I no longer worried about Dad and Cosmic Cosmo fighting, I called Sage to tell her about how and where we found him.

Sage sounded concerned when she answered her cell. "This is Sage."

I relayed my information to her quickly. "Good news. We have Cosmic Cosmo. Dad found him just as we were ready to leave and help you look. When Dad opened our front door, he found Cosmic Cosmo sitting on our front door mat, purring like a kitten. He let Dad pick him up and snuggled with him."

Sage sounded happy. "I can never thank

you enough. I'll be right over with his kennel to retrieve my little bad boy. He gave me quite a scare."

I hung up and told Dad. "Sage is on her way to get him."

It took mere minutes for Sage to pull into our driveway. After all, she did live that close. Dad heard her car and stepped outside, holding Cosmic Cosmo. When Sage saw Dad holding her buddy, she had love in her eyes for the two of them. "Kyle, thank you. I don't understand why he would come here. Anyway, I brought his kennel."

She opened the back door of her SUV and pulled it out. When she approached Cosmic Cosmo with it, he hissed. She sounded surprised. "What's this? I'm the hand who feeds you and takes care of you."

Dad caressed the cat's head. "It's okay, buddy. You know Sage, I can't blame him. He's been penned up at the clinic for almost two weeks. I was the only one brave enough to take him out of his cage every day and hold him. My staff was afraid of getting scratched or bit. How about you take a deep breath and come inside for a coffee or hot chocolate?"

Sage, relieved, replied. "That would be nice, but how about Chester?"

"Luci put him in her bedroom and closed the door. I think we can keep them apart."

Sage smiled, put the kennel back, and locked her car before we all went inside. I was worried about Cosmic Cosmo meeting our Christmas tree, but Dad had everything under control. He held onto that purring cat while Sage looked at our decorations. "What a beautiful Christmas tree. You have an angel on top as well."

Dad smiled. "Thank you. Luci's our decorator. Please follow us into the kitchen. Good thing Luci cleaned up. The dinner you sent home with us was as great tonight as it was last night. Would you like coffee, tea, or hot chocolate?"

"Hot chocolate sounds wonderful even in seventy-five degree heat," she laughed.

I added. "I'll take care of that, Dad, if you take care of Cosmic Cosmo."

I put the kettle on and got out our Christmas mugs and a holiday platter to put some cookies one of Dad's patients sent us in a pretty tin. Dad sat with Cosmic Cosmo on his lap. Sage sat next to Dad. I glanced over at them. They looked so happy. Dad held Cosmic Cosmo while Sage petted him and smiled at Dad.

I put a doily on the plate and arranged some cookies before I placed red paper napkins and green paper plates on the table. When the water boiled, I made three cups of hot chocolate and added marshmallows. I couldn't believe how good Chester was. He stayed quiet in my room and didn't whine.

We drank our hot chocolate and ate some cookies as Dad and Sage chatted the entire time, mostly about Christmas when they were kids. Dad began. "You know I moved to Florida to attend veterinary school. I grew up in upstate New York. My friends and I went sledding after we opened our gifts and always had a blast."

Sage laughed. "Small world sometimes. I grew up in New Jersey. We always went to church on Christmas Eve and to my grandmother's on Christmas Day after we opened our gifts to share holiday fun with aunts, uncles, and cousins. More gifts followed, after which we enjoyed the best Christmas dinner on the planet."

Sounded like happy times for both. We finished our treats, and Dad turned to Sage. "Let me put Cosmic Cosmo in his kennel and take him home for you in my car. When we get there, I'll help get him settled. He's never been to your new home and isn't used to the new surroundings. That's most likely why he came to find me. I'm familiar to him. I advise my pet parents to let your pet move in with you and see you unpacking, but that presents other problems, especially if you have one as active as my man C.C. here."

Sage nodded. "I didn't think of that.

You're right. He probably wasn't aware that he was at home." She looked at me. "Luci, thank you for this. I didn't have any dessert tonight, so this was quite a treat." I smiled, happy Cosmic Cosmo was safe, and Sage liked my dessert.

Dad interrupted my thoughts. "Okay, gang, let's get going." I watched from our front window as Dad carried C.C., took the kennel out of Sage's car with his free hand, and put it in his back seat. He gently coaxed Cosmic Cosmo inside. Sage walked close behind. She leaned in and put her head on his shoulder before she left in her own car.

Since Chester needed his nightly walk, I followed the two cars on foot. I got to Sage's right after they did. I waved to Sage as she unlocked her front door. Sage returned the wave, asking, "Luci, want to come in?"

I shook my head 'no' and pointed to Chester. "I'll wait out here to see how Cosmo reacts." Sage nodded while Dad carried Cosmic Cosmo in his kennel and followed her inside.

Sage's living room had those large front

windows, so I could see Dad kneel in front of the couch and open the kennel. He took Cosmic Cosmo out of his kennel and held him for a few seconds before he put him down. No cries for help. No damaged Christmas tree, so Dad must have been right. Sage then walked Dad outside. She made a sudden stop on her front step, which made Dad stop. She reached for something from behind her back, looked at me, and winked. I heard a jingle as she whipped out a piece of mistletoe with jingle bells, held it over Dad's head, and gave him a sweet kiss on the cheek in front of the blinking Christmas lights of her wreath. Her kiss could have come right out of a holiday movie. Dad's face turned as red as Rudolph's nose. He smiled at Sage before he smiled at me, a bit embarrassed, but I could still tell he liked it.

"Okay, you two ready to go home?" he asked as Chester and I jumped into his back seat. Dad continued to chatter, probably hoping I'd forget about that kiss. "Sage is sure nice and a lot of fun. That Cosmic Cosmo's quite a character. She told me someone abandoned him in a box in a field. He wasn't very old but would hunt for food since his rescuers found dead field mice around his lair. When Sage saw him in the shelter, she fell in love with him at once and wanted to give him a good home. I hope that dang cat knows how lucky he is. Speaking of lucky, how did our Chester do on his nightly quest?"

"Good Dad, and don't worry, I cleaned up after him."

Chester and I followed Dad inside to say goodnight, but he was very chatty and still sounded too excited to go to sleep. "I can't wait to take you and Sage to the auction tomorrow night! We're all going to have a wonderful time."

With that, he kissed me goodnight and went to his bedroom. Wow! I've never seen him this excited...about an auction we attend every year.

CHAPTER EIGHT

From the first second I opened my eyes, all I could think about was how happy I was to go to the holiday charity auction tonight with Dad, Chester, and Sage. I stretched my arms as far up in the air as I could before peeking at Chester, who was still asleep. I snuck out of bed, hoping not to disturb Chester and looked out my window. It was raining, and the air near my window felt damp, so I grabbed my fluffy pink robe and strolled into the kitchen. Dad was already dressed in shorts and a T-shirt and on the phone. I stopped to listen. He must be talking to Sage because I heard him say:

"I'm looking forward to seeing you tonight as well." He turned and shot me a smile. "Looks like sleepyhead Luci just woke up, and what's this? Here comes a groggy Chester. I'm going to have to run. I want to make Luci breakfast this morning. She always makes mine. See you at four-thirty." Dad hung up and looked at me.

"That was Sage. She called to thank us. Cosmic Cosmo, or as I like to call him, C.C., is adjusting to his new home, and she wanted us to know how much she appreciated our help in finding him. What can I make my sleepyhead angel for breakfast? Waffles? Pancakes? Scrambled eggs? "

I smiled. Dad was way too cute. I knew his specialty was scrambled eggs, but I thought he needed a break. "Thanks, but I'm fine with toast and peanut butter."

"You realize you're making this too easy for me. Not fair." Dad laughed. Since he had already made his coffee, he placed my two pieces of whole wheat bread in the toaster. "You know, that sounds pretty good. I think I'll have the same."

We enjoyed everything about breakfast,

especially spending time together. Dad revealed, "You know Mattie from my staff. Well, she found an abandoned puppy yesterday so cute that when she returned to the clinic with him, everyone in the waiting room wanted to take the pup home. I sure didn't want to hurt any of my patients' feelings, so I advised them that anyone interested in adopting him would find him at the island shelter. The shelter staff would decide. Anyway, I named the puppy Casanova because of the way women swooned over him." We got a chuckle out of his choice of names.

Later that day, after Chester and I returned from our afternoon walk, we passed by Dad's bedroom. His door was open, so we peeked in. We noticed he had placed his wedding ring on the dresser in front of Mom and Dad's wedding photo. The gold ring sparkled in the small ray of sunlight streaming in from his window. I don't understand why he would take off his ring? He never did that before. Maybe he wanted to clean it? It reminded me of the time when his sister, my Aunt Clare, visited and asked him why he still wore the ring after all these years. He said, "To remember my Julia and never forget all the wonderful moments of love we shared."

I never asked Dad about that conversation or why he took it off today. I didn't want to add to his pain, so I went to my room, showered and changed for the auction.

We all wanted to look our best for Sage, but Dad really killed it. Handsome as ever in navy shorts and a blue and white Hawaiian shirt, I noticed he still wasn't wearing his wedding ring. That alone was odd, but as I said, I did not want to ask him why.

I wore my favorite pink shorts and striped top. Chester was all set in a new turquoise collar with pictures of tropical fish on it, appropriate for a fish fry. One of Dad's patients gave it to him. We left to pick up Sage. When we arrived, Chester and I hung out in the backseat as Dad went to her front door and knocked. Sage came out looking amazing in a sleeveless mint green sundress with a short sleeve white jacket.

As soon as we arrived at the waterfront restaurant, we could hear a band playing country western dance music. Since Dad bought our dinner tickets ahead, our server guided us around the ticket table, and all the couples dancing to a table outside near the commercial fishing docks we could share with Chester. It had stopped raining and turned into a beautiful, cool evening with a full moon shimmering on the bay waters.

White Christmas lights strung around the posts near the outside seating twinkled while many of the fishing boats flashed multi-colored holiday lights.

Dad looked at his watch. "Okay, who's ready for some fresh fish? Think I'll go put our dinner orders in. I can tell my two shoppers don't want to miss a single minute of bidding."

Dad went to the window of the open kitchen and handed our tickets to a server. He returned shortly with a plastic number on a stand. Our server followed and brought us two glasses of white wine and my root beer before surprising me with a bowl of water for Chester. It did not take too much longer for our dinners to arrive. We each devoured the four large pieces of fresh Gulf fish, cole slaw, and hush puppies in silence like we had never eaten fresh fish before. We cleaned our plates. Yummy didn't do it justice.

After dinner, Sage told us about her first fishing trips as a little girl with her Dad. The three of us laughed so loud we made the people at the tables nearest ours laugh, too. She told us. "My dad loved to fish and wanted me to like it as much as he did, so he bought me a small child's fishing pole and reel. I tried and tried all that morning to catch a fish. I was excited when I finally caught a couple, but they looked extra small to me compared to Dad's catch. Dad smiled as he took them off the hook for me and put them in his catch bag. While my dad's friend Tony distracted me, I learned when I was older that Dad had fooled me and released them because they *were* too small. My mom waited for our return, ready to cook all the fish we caught for dinner. When I came into the kitchen, I saw only big fish in her huge frying pan. The look on my face must have said it all because Dad then told me, "You know, Sage, fish get bigger when you fry them." I trusted my dad so much and was so naïve I believed that story through most of grade school.

We laughed because the story was as cute as she was. She kept going. "Another time, Dad and I went fishing with this high school athlete who was our neighbor and the hunkiest boy I had ever seen by the time I was eleven. I wanted to impress him, so I cast the line over my shoulder only to catch the hook in the seat of my pants. Talk about an embarrassing moment." The more Sage told us about herself, the more we loved her.

My schoolmate and neighbor Ashley, who sat at a nearby outside table, saw us and came over to say 'hello.' I introduced her to everyone. "Ashley, you already know my dad and Chester, but I'd like you to meet Ms.

Domano, our new head librarian."

Ashley gushed. "I'm so happy to meet you. I don't have a reading dog like Chester, but I do come early to set up the chairs and select a book I think the kids would love."

Sage beamed. "I appreciate that and can't wait to greet everyone involved with the reading dog program." Just as she finished that statement, the band changed pace and began to play slow country music as we watched couples near us get up to dance on the dock. Dad stood and looked into Sage's eyes.

"Since we can't shop for another thirty minutes, would my lady care for a dance?"

Sage smiled and nodded as he took her hand, helped her stand, and escorted her onto the dock. Ashley became curious. "They make such a sweet couple. Are they dating?"

I responded. "No, they just became friends."

Ashley retorted. "I'm too young to know about romance, but I watch a lot of sweet holiday romance movies, and those two are definitely into each other. They look so natural and happy together. I've never seen your dad smile so much. He's always so serious."

We watched as Dad put his arm around Sage's waist while she put her arms around his neck. As they danced, they stared into each other's eyes like they were the only couple on the dance floor. Ashley sighed. "Gosh, your dad is so handsome and Ms. Domano so beautiful. They look like my paper dolls. Your dad sure looks like he's enjoying this dance."

As the music became slower, we watched Dad pull Sage closer to him before he twirled her around and dipped her back in his arms.

Their eyes fixed on each other's, they swayed to the music. I tried not to stare but was so thrilled to see him this happy. Chester, seated under the table, wagged his tail like crazy. Ashley kept us company until the music stopped. The band announced a break. Dad put a tip in their coffee can before he and Sage came back to the table.

As if right on que, the doors to the auction

room opened. Ashley and I clapped. Dad then gave Sage a quick lay of the land on how this auction worked before we entered. "Go into the auction room and look at everything before you decide to bid. You can bid now, but remember we'll go in again fifteen minutes before the auction closes to firm up our bids. Okay Luci, Sage? Ashley, would you like to come with us?"

Ashley shook her head 'no' before responding. "I'm waiting to go inside with my mom and dad."

Dad then gave us the battle cry. "Ready, set, shop!"

There were so many wonderful donations it was hard not to bid on them all. By the end of the night, Sage bought Dad's gift certificate for Cosmic Cosmo, a deep blue glass dish with dolphins painted on it, and a book about fish found in the Gulf of Mexico for me. It came with a pretty blue carry bag with a fish design. Dad scooped up as many restaurant gift certificates as he could. He liked to give them out as holiday gifts, but for some odd reason, I think he may use them himself this year. I wasn't old enough to bid, but Dad bought me a hand beaded bracelet in pink and lavender that I liked.

Everyone happy with our purchases, we left for home. On the way, I asked. "Dad, please drop us off in our driveway so Chester and I can take a short walk, and he can do his nightly business."

Dad paused, "But we drive right by Sage's house, so let me drop Sage off first." When we arrived at Sage's, I watched Dad open the car door for her, take hold of her bags, and walk her to her front door. They lingered quite a while. Dad put her bags down as they stared into each other's eyes. Sage gave him a hug before I was surprised to hear her say. "Kyle, thank you for a fun evening. I hope you know how much I love spending time with you and Luci."

Dad smiled. "Funny, we feel the exact same way about you. Glad you could join us.

Goodnight Sage." She gave him another big hug before he kissed the tip of her nose, handed her the bags, and walked to his car and us. He looked so happy and hummed "Jingle Bells" all the way home.

When Chester and I returned from our walk, Dad gave me a quick kiss goodnight and said, "Luci, you're the best daughter anyone could ever have." With that, he went to his room.

After I changed into my nightshirt and put Chester's old collar back on, we sat on the bed and talked like we often did. Well, really, I did all the talking. Chester just listened. "Hey, buddy, do you think Sage is the answer to Mom's visit and my Wishing Cookie?" When I looked over at him, Chester was sound asleep, so I stood and sent my nightly hug to Mom. My eyelids felt so heavy that I fell asleep as soon as my head hit my pillow. I wasn't asleep for very long when that same bright light that had filled my room before startled me awake. I sat up and shaded my eyes with my hands so I could better see that beautiful vision of my mom. Chester didn't growl this time. He whimpered and rolled over on his back.

Mom looked as beautiful as before. Her touch warmed my face, and I felt that warmth flow through my entire body as Mom's spirit began to speak to me. Her voice was so soft I wasn't at all frightened this time. "Luci, my darling child, I've been watching you and am very proud of the young lady you've become. My spirit took the form of that cardinal that led you to Sage's house. You guessed correctly. She *is* the answer to your Wishing Cookie, but I must warn you. You are the keeper of that wish. I know that's a lot for a thirteen-year-old girl to understand, but I'm confident you can make their love work. You must respect your wish, honor your commitment, and make their relationship grow stronger with each passing day.

"Human feelings are very fragile, and relationships can fall apart at any time. Please be aware of that. That will happen in the near future to Dad and Sage. When it does, help mend their broken hearts so they stay in love and together. I am confident you can and will do just that.

"Since your wish has been granted and my work here is almost done, I'm leaving you for a short time. Please remember I'll always love you and Dad very much and will always be with you. Whenever you need my guidance, call out to me, and I'll return to help you. No tears, please, we'll see each other again soon and as I already told you, keep those wonderful hugs coming my way."

With that, she blew me a kiss. Her kiss left a trail of tiny shimmering bright white lights that exploded all over my room right before everything went dark. I sat there in shock, stunned that she would leave me so soon. I called out, "Mom. Mom, please don't go," hoping she would return. I so wanted to feel more of her love I longed for and missed my entire life, but I was too late. She had already vanished, and my tear-filled cries became loud enough to wake Dad.

Dad, his hair ruffled, looked like I startled him awake. He rushed into my room and couldn't ask me fast enough. "Luci, are you okay? I heard your cries from my room."

He walked over and sat next to me on my bed, kissing my forehead and hugging me as tight as he could. I felt tears streaming down his cheeks as he comforted me. "Honey, please don't cry. You must have had a dream because I heard you call out for Mom. You and I miss her so. I only wish you had a chance to meet her and get to know her. She can't be with you in person, but I truly believe she hears you and is always with you. Her love for us, like ours for her, will never die."

Chester sensed something was wrong with me and tried to squeeze in the middle of our hug. Dad smiled. "Your buddy sure looks out for you. Would you like me to stay here until you and Chester fall back to sleep?"

I nodded and fell asleep, wondering when and if I'd see Mom again with Chester snuggling next to me and Dad holding my hand.

CHAPTER NINE

I shielded my eyes from the sun's bright morning rays, disappointed they weren't from Mom's spirit. I heard noises coming from the kitchen, so I knew Dad was already up. As soon as I walked in, he greeted me with a big kiss on my cheek. "Guess what, Luci, I'm free all day, no calls or, as of yet, no emergencies."

I smiled. "Dad, that's great. Thanks for last night. I love you." I gave him a big hug. "It'll be a treat to have you home all day. We'll have to celebrate. I think I'll make blueberry pancakes from the mix Meta gave me after I take Chester for a quick walk? How does that sound?"

Dad's ear to ear grin answered my question, so when we returned, I made pancakes. Dad said in between bites, "Hmmm, what a great way to start my day. You make the best pancakes. I've had a long two weeks of work with no break, so today, I'm going to catch up on my favorite football games. I'll start with the pre-game shows and follow up with as many games as I can squeeze in. Luci, I hope you can watch some with me."

I nodded. "I'd like that, Dad. Maybe I can make us some popcorn later." He gave me two thumbs up before he left for the living room and his pregame shows.

I took Chester out for his second walk of the morning. We didn't go far, only to Meta's house. I hadn't seen her in a few days and wanted to check up on her. As usual, she was delighted to see us. "You have perfect timing. My family just left for that pirate ship ride in the Gulf this morning, so I'm alone for the next few hours. How's your dad doing?"

Chester and I went inside and sat at her kitchen table. "He's fine."

Meta beamed when she saw us. "Lately,

every time I see him, he has a big smile on his face and looks so happy, almost like there's someone new in his life. Have you and your dad met our new neighbor, Sage?" She smiled like she knew the answer to her question already.

I answered. "We have, and as you probably guessed, they're spending time together as friends. We all are."

Meta nodded. "I'm very happy to hear that. Sage is very nice and brought me some Italian Christmas cookies when she stopped by to introduce herself. Please let your dad know I'm not forgetting about our traditional Christmas dinner. After all, you're my beach family. My son's family will still be here to celebrate with us. Please invite Sage and bring Chester."

"Christmas dinner for that many people is a lot of work for you, Meta, but you know I'll help any way I can," I replied.

"Thank you, but treating my big family will be my pleasure. Have you had breakfast yet?" Meta asked.

I nodded. "I made the blueberry pancake mix you gave me." My response made Meta chuckle.

"You are becoming quite the chef. That's good you ate because we now have time for sweets." Meta pulled out a tin with small chocolate wafers, and we each enjoyed two.

Chester and I stayed at Meta's for a short while longer. When we got back home, Dad was watching his first game. I sat on the arm of his chair and put my head on his shoulder. I love it when he stays home with me.

He waited for the commercial before he sounded excited to tell me. "Luci, I just read in the Beach Times that our local theater company is performing "It's A Wonderful Life," the Christmas black and white movie classic, as a radio show. The performance will be in the rec center for one night only on the 23rd. I know you've never seen the movie and have no idea what home entertainment was like before color TV, internet streaming, and video games, so this could be a fun way for you to learn about recent history. I was thinking about inviting Sage. I have a short day on the 23rd, and the clinic is closed except for emergencies on Christmas Eve and Day. Think the 23rd would work for everyone?"

"Sounds like fun," I replied. "That would be great, Dad. Can we go to the Island ice cream parlor for ice cream sodas afterwards?"

"You mean the one where 'Every Day is a Sundae'? That's a date I'm always happy to keep."

I blurted out. "Oh, before I forget. I checked up on Meta earlier, and she wants us to keep our tradition of Christmas dinner at her house. She said she would love for us, her beach family, to celebrate with her visiting family. Sage is welcome, too, so please ask her. I already volunteered to help Meta because she'll have such a big group. It'll be so much fun. I can't wait."

~*~

The night of our holiday show finally

arrived. I couldn't wait to see it because I had never even heard of old-time radio shows, as Dad called them, or how they worked. I dressed in a rose colored sun dress before I fed Chester and walked him around the yard.

Dad came into the kitchen wearing a light green fishing shirt, even though he doesn't fish and shorts, but I noticed he still wasn't wearing his wedding ring. Again, not wanting to upset him, all I could say was, "Wow, Dad, you look like a beach hunk."

That put a big smile on his face. "Well, this beach hunk thinks it's time to get Sage, so let's go."

When we arrived at Sage's, Dad's eyes followed her from the second she came out of her front door to the time she reached our car. She looked that beautiful. Dressed in a pale yellow flowered sundress with a white shawl, she smiled at Dad as he got out and opened the car door for her. Once comfy, she greeted us. "Hi, you two great looking people. This should be fun. And ice cream sodas afterwards? I haven't had one of those in years. I'm so glad you accepted my invitation for Christmas Eve dinner. You know Chester's always welcome. I'll have C.C. in his kennel so he doesn't misbehave."

The play was so much fun. The cast did an amazing job. I imagined people sitting at home listening to shows on their tall wooden radios like the one that sat on our side of the stage. Talented actors read more than one role while one of them made sound effects such as a door closing or footsteps using props. The set was decorated to look like the on-air room of a radio station at Christmas time. Green garlands with colored lights hung from the rafters while loads of potted poinsettias lined the stage. Our program stated the flowers would be distributed to the local senior center after the show. I thought that was nice.

The actors all wore colorful holiday costumes in red, green, and plaids. When I admired the dresses during the fifteen-minute intermission, Dad told me. "You know Luci, they were in style in the 1940's. Pretty snazzy, huh?"

"Snazzy?" I asked. "Is that a word from back then, too?"

Dad laughed. "The actresses look beautiful with hairdos and make-up to match that time. The actor with the pin-striped suit and the red bow tie has the perfect low-pitched voice to be MC, and that talented lady who sat on a stool next to him sang all those commercials for products I bet you don't recognize." Dad was right; I didn't recognize any of them. I did remember my grandma, Dad's Mom, telling me how she loved to listen to those old radio shows with her family when she was a little girl, but I never realized how much work went into making them until tonight.

The MC greeted as many audience members as possible during intermission. When he came to us, Dad asked. "May I take a photo of you with my daughter Luci?' He nodded, and Dad snapped a photo with his cell. Dad was right. I had never seen the movie, but this year, I loved the play so much that I plan to do so. That George Bailey was quite a guy. Intermission over, Dad took Sage's hand to hold when the show started again. I pretended not to see that. I so wanted them to be happy. This wonderful holiday show ended to a standing ovation. On our way out, all of the actors lined up to greet us and gave everyone a candy cane. How nice was that? I made out like a bandit because Sage and Dad gave me theirs.

Next stop: "I Love Ice Cream Where Every Day is a Sundae." That popular ice cream shop was so busy we had to wait for a table. I think everyone on the island who went to the show had the same idea. We sat outside on a picnic table while we waited for our turn to order. It was a clear night with too many twinkling stars to count. Dad already guessed what each of us wanted. "Luci, a vanilla soda with pistachio ice cream. Sage, a chocolate soda with chocolate fudge ice cream and mine will be the same as Sage's." He sure knew how to make us happy. Almost everyone in that small shop stopped by our table to say "hi" to Dad. They all loved him because he took such good care of their family's "fur balls of love," as I liked to call them.

Our ice cream sodas slurped to the very bottom of our glasses, we walked to our car. All the way, Dad had one arm around my shoulder and one around Sage's. Before we got into the car, Dad turned to Sage and said. "I'm sure I can speak for both of us. Just knowing you brighten our lives and makes us happy. This is the merriest Christmas I've had in a long time."

Sage leaned in to nuzzle Dad's cheek. "It is for me, too. Thank you for all the fun and joy you've brought into my life." She turned to face me. "And thanks for sharing Luci. I adore this young lady. She's the daughter anyone would love to have."

Wow! I didn't expect to hear that! When we reached Sage's, she took hold of Dad's hand. "Would you like to come in for a quick nightcap, maybe coffee, maybe root beer?"

Dad smiled as he stared into her eyes.

I interrupted his thoughts. "I should go home and take care of Chester, but Dad, please go inside and enjoy some coffee."

I could tell my response surprised Dad. "Are you sure? Will you be all right?"

I nodded. "I'll be fine. Thanks, Sage, for the invitation, but by this time, Chester needs his walk. See you Christmas Eve. I'm looking forward to it."

I got out of our car and started to walk home, hoping if I left them alone, the magic of Christmas love would grow deeper between them. I heard a noise and looked up to see that beautiful red cardinal fly out of a nearby hibiscus bush bursting with red flowers. He circled my path before he turned back. My eyes followed him as he landed on a palm tree branch near Sage's front door. I heard happy chatter coming from that direction and followed him, wanting to see what was happening. I saw Sage kiss Dad's cheek as she held up that same branch of Mistletoe over Dad's head.

She dropped the Mistletoe, and they hugged. They looked so happy I left and continued to walk home, content that Mom's magic and my Wishing Cookie were working!

When I returned home, I went inside, put on Chester's leash, and started to take Chester for his nightly walk just as Dad pulled into our driveway. He smiled and hummed "Jingle Bells" again. When he turned to get out of his car, I spotted a blotch of red lipstick, the same color Sage wore on his cheek. Dad walked over to us and kissed the top of my head. "Luci, you know how much I love you. Nothing will ever change that. I had so much fun tonight watching your reactions to the show and answering all of your questions. And the ice cream sodas were the best idea ever!"

He gave me the biggest hug before he went inside. Chester and I stayed outside to finish our walk. I looked up at the star-filled night sky, hoping my wish for Sage and Dad would come true and that I would see my mom's beautiful spirit again.

CHAPTER TEN

Christmas Eve: I loved to celebrate the Eve as much as Christmas Day. I wrapped my presents, decorated my cards, and tried as hard as I could to keep Chester from finding his holiday treats. Dad and I have always celebrated alone. He would order two prime rib dinners from one of our fancier island restaurants with all the trimmings, salad, baked potato, asparagus, and gravy. We enjoyed peppermint stick ice cream with fudge sauce for dessert. But tonight, we'll be celebrating in a new and different way at Sage's. I was so happy because I adored her, so anything she cooked for us was fine with me.

I wrapped two presents I bought for Dad after saving up my allowance and made Sage a snowman card from my kit using scraps of lace, sequins, and glitter. I put a snapshot of Chester and me inside that Dad had printed from his computer. I also bought her a cute, chubby snowwoman decoration for her tree I hoped to give her tonight. I then wrapped more gifts I planned to give both her and Dad tomorrow.

Dad called out right before we were supposed to leave. "I'll be right back, honey. I want to pick up a couple of things to bring to Sage's." He was gone about twenty minutes only to return with a dozen red roses in a holiday vase and a bottle of white wine called Pinot Grigio. Sage told us she invited us to share the Feast of the Seven Fishes with her. It was an Italian tradition on Christmas Eve from her family's region in southern Italy. Being an islander, I love seafood, so we should be in for a treat.

When we arrived, Sage greeted us at the door. "Kyle, Luci, and Chester, I'm so happy to share Christmas Eve with you. Look at those gorgeous red roses. Thank you. I'll place them on the side cabinet so we can all enjoy looking at them during dinner." Dad showed her the wine. "Kyle, your choice of wine once again is perfect!"

When we stepped inside, I noticed all the new decorations she added since I was there last. The dining room table was set as before, with holiday dishes and a poinsettia tablecloth, while her side cabinets had different size snowmen sitting on top of white cotton snow.

We all followed her into the dining room as she continued to tell us about the menu. "This is a traditional Italian holiday meal. I cooked all day and didn't make any appetizers tonight, so you can save room to devour all this fresh seafood. After we're seated, I'll explain the feast's original menu and origin. I did make some adjustments to the menu because I didn't care for squid and eel, among other things." I shuddered after hearing that but was relieved to learn she made changes to the menu. Sage escorted us to the holiday table. "Please find your snowman and be seated."

She was so cute she made snowmen out of Styrofoam balls, each holding a sign with a name and decorated differently. Mine had a pink hat and shawl, Dad's a blue sweater, and Sage's held a small green and red wreath. When I sat down, Chester lay down in the corner behind me. Dad uncorked the wine and filled their glasses before asking, "Sage, where may I find Luci's root beer?" Sage must be part mind reader because she came out from the kitchen with the bottle in her hand.

First course, Sage brought out a Caesar salad. As we enjoyed our salads, she began to explain this traditional holiday eve dinner. "'Festadi sette Pesci' is a Christmas Eve tradition in Southern Italy because its coastline is abundant with fish. The Feast began as a break from a day of religious fasting. In the early 1900s, immigrants from that region brought the feast to the US to make them feel closer to their homeland. As I said before, I narrowed down the menu that included squid, cod called baccala, eel, mussels, anchovies, shrimp, and scallops, to my three favorites: Shrimp Scampi over linguini with our locally caught pink shrimp, Grouper Francaise instead of cod, and baked scallops with a crusty cheesy topping. My grandmother brought the tradition here with her from Naples, and we continue to honor her memory by cooking a version of her original Feast every Christmas Eve. My mother told me it was okay to adapt the menu to my liking, so I did. Once we finish our salads, I'll bring out my version of the Feast."

Salads eaten, Dad stood and followed Sage into the kitchen to help carry out the three large serving platters filled with our main courses. Chester was so good. He lifted his nose to sniff the aromas coming from the platters before he placed his head back down in his paws. Everything was so delicious. We all had seconds of our favorite. Mine was the shrimp and pasta.

Dad rubbed his stomach. "Sage, that meal was beyond amazing. I loved every bite of it. Can't you tell? My waistline expanded at least two inches."

She laughed. "Glad you both enjoyed it. We'll take a break before we have dessert. Maybe once I clear the table, we can sit and talk."

I was eager to ask. "Sage, may I help you with the dishes and put the food away?" She smiled and nodded, so I helped Sage clear before we sat down again. Once seated, I pulled my card and small gift from my pocket and gave it to her. After Sage opened them, a big smile spread across her face. "Luci, this card is so beautiful. You know how much I love snowmen, and they're standing in all that sparkling snow... and this cute snowwoman for my tree? Thank you. I'm going to name her Luci with an 'i' and frame your photo with Chester to give it a place of honor on my bookcase hall of fame." Her last statement made me really happy.

My stomach couldn't wait for our next course...dessert. Sage served gelato with homemade biscotti. My gelato was pistachio, while theirs was chocolate. I couldn't help but notice the loving looks Dad and Sage shared. He talked in between bites of his biscotti. "Sage, you already know Meta invited all of us to Christmas dinner at 2 p.m. Please come to our house at noon to share a Christmas celebration with Luci and me."

Sage grinned. "I'd love to."

Dad did the watch thing. I knew that meant time to go. "Dad, why don't you stay a few minutes longer? I'll walk Chester home so he gets his nightly walk." Dad agreed, so I thanked Sage, gave her the biggest hug I could, and left.

Dad didn't stay too much longer than I did, nowhere near as long as I hoped. By the time I attached Chester's leash, and we began to walk down Sage's driveway, I heard them laughing by her front door. I turned to wave just as I saw Dad take Sage's hands and lean in for a quick kiss. They knew Chester and I were there because Sage smiled and waved as soon as they let go of that kiss. Sage then shot me a wink and had a mischievous smile before she grabbed Dad by his shirt collar and pulled him toward her for another quick kiss. Wow! This is getting serious. I headed for home, not wanting to interrupt their newfound happiness.

~*~

On Christmas morning, Dad and I opened our gifts like we always did after a holiday breakfast of toasted orange cranberry bread and juice. He loved the golf balls I gave him and even liked the great smelling shower gel I had picked out for him. Dad spoiled me with a new pale blue flowered sundress, two new video games, and some bubble bath and fancy soaps. Chester got his favorite treats and a new squeaky octopus to chase around the house. We cleaned up the wrappings before Sage arrived. On time, she walked over to our house and carried in two large holiday gift bags, each tied together with multi-colored ribbons.

Once Sage was inside and comfortable, Dad made them cappuccino and brought me another glass of juice. Sage placed the gift bags on the floor nearest her seat. When she saw Chester sniffing one of the bags, Sage laughed. "Luci, I think you should open your gift first since nosey Chester's gift is in there as well."

Sage stood and handed me my bag. I loved everything in it, and so did Chester. Sage gave me a book about the movie "It's A Wonderful Life" with black and white photos of the cast and scenes from the movie. While in another box wrapped in snowman paper, I discovered a pretty pink blouse with a lace collar and a pink sequined necklace.

I gushed. "Sage, thank you so much! I can't wait to read the book, and the blouse and necklace are so pretty. I'm going to wear them on New Year's Eve!" Chester found special treats from the doggie bakery in town and a new orange tennis ball. His tail wouldn't stop wagging.

Dad's bag was next. Fancy cologne and a new golf shirt I already knew about because Sage asked me his size last week. It was Sage's turn. She loved her gifts. I gave her a pewter keychain with a cat on it, a box of fudge, and a cat toy for C.C., as we call him. Dad surprised me because he said he hadn't bought a gift for a woman except for Grandma since Mom died. He gave Sage perfume and a long royal blue silk scarf with deep rose hibiscus on it and emerald green leaves. Sage, who looked beautiful in an emerald green dress, said. "Kyle, this is so lovely. I'm going to wear it to Meta's. Thank you."

Presents open, we loaded our next batch of goodies for our favorite neighbor. Sage bought Meta an apron with "World's Best Baker" on it. I made Meta a card, and Dad bought two bottles of wine and a pretty pot of white poinsettias.

We enjoyed Christmas dinner with Meta's family. Josh, her son, laughed, saying, "Mom made us all try her magical Swedish Wishing Cookies, but none of ours broke apart the right way." Meta winked at me, so I remained silent.

We filled our stomachs with turkey,

ham, and all the traditional trimmings. Meta baked so many desserts that if I were to taste one of each, I'd be there all night. We were like one big happy family and loved spending Christmas together. Meta took Sage's hand before we were about to leave and said, "Sage, please don't be a stranger. We only live a few houses apart. You're always welcome here."

Sage smiled and kissed her cheek. "Thank you, Meta. I'll remember that if you remember my door is always open for you. Your dinner made my first Christmas in my new hometown extra special."

We hugged and thanked everyone and left. Dad and Sage left a few minutes ahead of us. As Chester, who had a great day with Meta's granddaughters, and I began to head down Meta's front walk to go back to our house, we saw Dad take Sage's hand. They stopped at the end of the walk, and I could hear Dad's voice tremble as he told Sage. "Thank you for a wonderful Christmas. Except for Luci's love over the past twelve holidays, Christmas was difficult to celebrate without Julia. You give our lives a new happiness and a new hope."

Sage smiled, quick to respond. "I know how you feel. I haven't celebrated with so much joy since I lost Brandon. You and Luci make me feel alive again."

I watched them hug and heard Dad laugh and Sage giggle. I've never seen my dad this happy. He gave Sage a sweet kiss on the cheek before they walked to Sage's under a beautiful star-filled sky. Dad came home a couple of hours later. Jingle Bells seemed to be his new whistle of choice.

The next morning, Chester and I were in our front yard playing with his new orange tennis ball. Dad had already left for work. Sage drove by and stopped. She motioned for me to come over and opened her car window. "Luci, I have to go in to the library for a few hours to get ready for my new job. Would you, Chester, and your dad like to come to lunch tomorrow?"

I hesitated. "That would be great, but tomorrow is my mom's birthday. We always take flowers to her grave to remember and honor her. It's a tough day for Dad and me."

Sage remained silent for a few minutes. "I understand how difficult a visit like that can be. I would visit Brandon's grave on his birthday every year before I moved here. I want you to know my door is always open, and I'd love to see you both."

I waved and called out as she drove away. "Hope to see you tomorrow Sage."

My thoughts about visiting Mom's grave carried with me to bedtime. I know how sad her birthday was for Dad. As I sent my special hug to Mom, I wondered if I'd see her beautiful spirit again. I missed her presence and wished we could have more time together, but I fell asleep thinking how lucky I was to have the best Dad, Meta, and now a new friend in Sage whom I cared about very much.

A few hours later, that surreal, bright, blinding light filled my room once again and startled me awake, but like the last time, I wasn't afraid. I welcomed her spirit. "Mom, it's your birthday tomorrow, and we're going to the cemetery like we do every year. I want you to know that even though we never met when you were alive, I love and miss you very much."

Her beautiful spirit touched my face. "And I miss and love you more than you can imagine my sweet angel, but tonight, I came to tell you that tomorrow is the day I warned you about. Your wish for Dad's and Sage's happiness will be tested. You'll need to mend two broken hearts in order to make your wish happen. I want you and Dad to have the happiness and love you deserve, and I know Sage will fill those needs, but there will be trouble between them. I trust you'll try your best to keep them together because of your love for both of them. Remember, I'll always be with you and Dad and love you both more than you can imagine."

With that, she blew me a kiss and just disappeared, and as she did, twinkling stars filled my room before it went dark. I didn't want her to leave, but what could I do? I know by Chester's expression he saw her, too. I hugged him, concerned about what kind of test would break apart my wish for Dad and Sage. It took a while, but we both fell back asleep until my human alarm clock, Dad, sounded. "Come on, Luci, get up. We're going to the cemetery in a little bit to visit Mom." He always spoke of her like she was still with us.

I dressed and attached Chester's leash, ready for our family outing. By the time I wandered into the kitchen, Dad had already left for the island florist to buy a dozen mauve roses, Mom's favorite, as he did every year. Lily, the florist, knew where we were going, so she always put them in a beautiful, unbreakable vase.

Dad and I ate a quick breakfast, after which I took care of Chester's morning duties. We left soon after that, happy to deliver flowers to Mom's grave as we did each year. Parking outside the small island cemetery, Dad took my hand, and we walked as slowly as if in a funeral procession to the cemetery's old black wrought iron gate decorated for the holiday with red silk poinsettia garlands. Dad pushed the gate open.

Our island cemetery lay on a piece of land off the main road. Mom's grave was not too far from the entrance gate. We knew where we were headed and stopped when we reached her rose-toned headstone carved with flowers that read "Julia Anne Mathews loving wife of Kyle and mother of Luci." Dad knelt, and I bowed my head as he placed the vase of flowers at the center of her headstone. He then kissed his left hand and touched her headstone. When he realized he wasn't wearing his wedding ring, he covered his eyes with his hands and started to sob.

"Julie, I'm sorry. I never wanted to hurt you or your memory. I'm so sorry I took off our ring. I promise I'll never take it off again, nor will I ever see another woman."

I touched his arm, hoping to console him. "Dad, please don't cry. You didn't do anything wrong. I'm sure Mom, more than anyone in this world, would want us to be happy, and if that means bringing Sage into our lives, I'm sure she would understand."

He covered his eyes again to hide his tears, but I could still see them stream down his cheeks. He kissed his fingers and touched her headstone again. "Julie, honey, I promise to make this right for you and for us. I'll never hurt you again as long as I live."

I knelt for a few minutes to give Mom my love and respect before we left for our car. I remained quiet the entire time because I promised Mom's spirit not to tell him about her visits.

Once we were inside the car, Dad paused. "I'm going to sit here for a few minutes to clear my mind and collect my thoughts about what to do to make my hurtful wrong to your mom right."

He looked over at me and paused for a few minutes. "Luci, I'm reluctant to tell you this, but the only way I can think of is to tell

Sage I can't see her anymore. I don't want to hurt Sage either. Luci, you're old enough and smart enough to know that I care about her very much, but not at the expense of dishonoring your mother's memory."

Chester, who had waited patiently for our return, leaned over Dad's seat and licked his cheek, trying to make him feel better. I wondered whether I should tell Dad about Sage's invitation. Maybe if he went there and saw Sage face to face, his feelings for her would make him feel better about their relationship. I touched his shoulder and spoke softly. "Dad, Sage invited us over after our visit to Mom's grave for a rest and to have something to eat."

An odd look crossed Dad's face. It was serious yet sad. "If we go to Sage's, I can make things right for your mom right away. How could I hurt her so by not wearing our wedding ring and dating someone else? What was I thinking?" Tears streamed down his cheeks once more as he sobbed. "I can't do that to her any longer."

I didn't want to ask what he meant by "make things right," but I could guess. I didn't know what to say or how to comfort him. My feelings became lost in his sadness. He started the car, and we shot straight over to Sage's like her house was on fire.

CHAPTER ELEVEN

Relieved we made it to Sage's in one piece, I watched Dad park in her driveway and remain silent in the car for a few minutes. He was face down on the steering wheel, his head in his hands, sobbing. I wanted to calm him, hoping he wouldn't do anything rash, but I still didn't know what to do. I tried to give him a hug, but he pushed me away.

Sage must have heard our car because she came out her front door to greet us. She smiled and waved for us to come inside. Dad saw her but didn't smile. He had the most serious expression on his face I have ever seen.

When we didn't get out of the car, Sage called out. "Kyle and Luci, I'm so glad you came. I'm sure you need a break. I know from personal experience how hard these moments can be. Come, sit, and unwind. I made a black and white cake and have chocolate ice cream for dessert after a light lunch."

Dad turned to me and said in the saddest tone, "Luci, you and Chester, wait here for me. Don't come after me, and don't try to put words in my mouth. I created this problem and must take care of it myself."

He got out and strode over to Sage, who, by this time, was standing in front of our car. I rolled down my window just enough so I could hear what they said. I heard Sage ask, "Kyle, you look terrible. What's wrong? Are Luci and Chester all right?"

With that, he took her hand, looked directly into her eyes, and spoke to her in the saddest tone. "Sage, you're a wonderful woman, but I can't see you anymore. I feel guilty every time we meet, like I'm dishonoring Julia's memory. I hope you'll understand and not hate me because of this. I certainly don't hate you." He covered his eyes with his free hand. "Quite the opposite, actually. I'm falling in love with you."

As he let go of Sage's hand, I saw a look of total shock and sadness cross her face before she started to cry. He kissed her forehead, turned, and left. Sage appeared so devastated she didn't look at Chester or me.

I was sad and devastated as well. Sage was the answer to my wish, and I know Dad cared for her as much as she cared for him. When they were together, they completed each other and made each other happy. Mom's spirit warned me something like this would happen and said I would have to fix it, but how? I'm only thirteen, so I knew I had to ask the wisest person I knew.

We arrived home at a much slower speed than when we left the cemetery. Chester and I followed Dad into the living room. He sat in his favorite recliner before I made him a cup of herbal tea. I asked, concerned. "Dad, you okay? Would you like something to eat?" He shook his head negatively and remained silent.

I knew better than to second-guess his actions. I didn't like it when someone did that to me, but I realized I had to get Dad talking if I wanted to get Sage and him back together.

Dad finished his tea and took a deep breath. "Luci, I'm going to lie down for a few minutes. I need a rest. I've had a very stressful morning."

I smiled and kissed his forehead. "I understand, Dad, and that may be the best thing for you to do. Do you need anything else?" He nodded "no."

"If you're all right, I may go see how Meta is? I haven't checked on her for a couple of days," I said.

Dad responded before he left for his room. "Give her my love and thank her again for Christmas."

Once Dad was settled, Chester and I left to visit the wisest person I have ever known in my entire life. I knocked on Meta's kitchen door only to hear her sweet voice respond. "Come in, Luci and Chester. I watched you come into my yard from my kitchen window."

When I opened the door this time, I was shocked to see her kitchen clean and in order. Meta laughed. "By the look on your face, I can tell you wonder if I had elves help me. Yes, I did, and they're named Greta and Anna, my granddaughters, who left with the rest of their family earlier this morning. I miss them already. Come sit. You look like something's bothering you, my child. What's wrong, Luci? Please sit with me and tell me all about it."

Meta could always read me like a book, so I sat next to her and began to tell her about my problem. "Meta, you met Sage. You know how nice she is and how happy she and Dad are together. Dad and I brought flowers to Mom's grave this morning, and Dad started to sob because he felt he had betrayed Mom's memory by not wearing his wedding ring and dating Sage. Sage had invited us over after our cemetery visit to help cheer us up. Dad drove us to Sage's, but instead of having our pain relieved, he broke up with her while Chester and I waited in the car. Of course, Sage was sad and cried. I want them to be happy but don't know what to do. How can I make Dad realize he made a big mistake? How can I make Sage forgive him? Meta, you're the wisest person I know, and I need your help more than you can imagine."

Meta shot me a grandmotherly smile and touched my hand. "Luci, first, you have to know I have handled many break-ups, but only between my kids. When they were young, they fought like cats and dogs, exclaiming they never wanted to see each other again. Since we're dealing with adults, I don't know if the method I used on my kids would work."

I sat up straight. "Meta, it may be worth a try. I'll do anything to bring them back together. I love Dad so much and want him to be happy. Sage is special to me as well. I'm sure my mom would approve."

I began to cry. Meta touched my shoulder and paused. "Luci, your mom was a generous and giving woman. I'm sure she only wants happiness for you and your dad."

She squeezed my hand. Her pale blue eyes twinkled as she shot me a kind smile. "Come on, we'll fix this together. Trust in my Wishing Cookie, and it will never let you down."

She paused for a few minutes. "Okay, let me remember how I handled my kids after they fought. The first thing I did was to find something my two boys shared in common; of those, which meant the most to each of them and could reunite their love as brothers. Do you know if your dad and Sage shared anything in common like that?"

I sighed, stumped by Meta's question, so I began to rattle off the first things that came to my mind. "They both lost someone they loved very much. Both love animals. Both like me." I made a funny face to show off that fact. "Sage is new to the island and needs help finding things or fixing things, but she did show me what she called her 'box of memories.' Things like keepsakes, photos, movie tickets, and menus from her special dates with Brandon, her late fiancé. Sage told me she liked to look at them and remember the happiness they shared."

"Does your dad have anything like that?" Meta asked.

I thought for a few seconds. "Yes, he does have a shoe box where he keeps memories of Mom. He brings out his 'memory box' every Saturday night to show me her photos and small keepsakes from their time together. He shares this with me, so I'll learn more about Mom. The last few times he opened this box, he kept fishing through it like something was missing. When I asked him about it, he said it was a letter Mom wrote to him on the day I was born. He said at the time, he didn't have the heart to open it and misplaced it shortly after Mom died. Sounded like it was very important to him, so since then, I've searched through dresser drawers and storage boxes, looking for it whenever I could, but as of yet, haven't found it."

"That's odd," Meta said. "Why would

your mother write him a letter when he's still there with her unless she thought she might die giving you birth. I was very sick once and wrote a letter to my eldest child in the event of my death. You said you looked through all kinds of stuff. Was that only in the house? Did you look in the garage as well? It may have ended up in a box with who knows what else and got buried in there. I've seen your garage." Meta chuckled.

"I looked in the garage as much as I could, but a lot of stuff is out of my reach, and I'm not sure about using a ladder in there with all the clutter, but for something this important, I suppose I could give it a try."

Meta nodded. "That's my girl. I know how much you care for your dad and Sage. If we want to help them, we must keep searching to find out what was in that letter."

I nodded. "You convinced me, Meta. Chester and I will take a look after we go home. Thank you for your help and understanding. I love you so much." I got up and hugged Meta before we left.

When I opened Meta's kitchen door, to my surprise, a red cardinal fluttered his wings and greeted Chester and me with a chirp from a nearby perch. My mind was filled with questions. Mom's spirit said she took the form of the cardinal and led us to Sage. Could he be Mom's spirit watching over us?

That cardinal followed us home and sat on a bush right outside our kitchen door. I went inside and did a quick check on Dad, who was still asleep, before heading into the garage. When Chester and I opened the side door to the garage, ready to go inside, that cardinal flew ahead of us and began to flutter and swoop back and forth like he was going crazy trying to find his way out. That couldn't be Mom's spirit. She was much too calm to act like that. Chester barked at him, and I left the door open for him to fly out the same way he came in, but for some odd reason, he flew by the open door and didn't leave.

I watched in awe as he flew to the very

upper shelves of the garage, striking boxes first to my left and then to my right until he centered his energy on a small cardboard box, hitting it more than once and knocking it off its shelf. The lid must not have been too secure because as the box fell, the lid came off, and all of the box's contents toppled onto the garage floor. Papers and small clothes scattered everywhere. When I dashed over to take a look at the mess that bird made, he flew out the open door. I rifled through the stuff to find all sorts of things from when I was a newborn: cards of congratulations, sympathy cards for Mom, and a couple of my baby clothes, which I thought Dad had donated. As I packed those things back into that box, I noticed a pale pink envelope. I held it in my hands and read, "To my dearest Kyle. Open only in the event of my death."

Since the box was only a little bigger than a shoe box, I brought everything inside. By that time, Dad was awake and in the living room watching TV. I walked over to him and handed him the box. I left that letter near the top so he would find it easily.

Dad looked puzzled, so I explained. "Dad, Chester and I went into the garage to look for something when this box fell from an upper shelf. As it fell, the lid came off, scattering papers and stuff all over the floor. When I looked through the contents, I thought you might like to see them."

As I showed him the cards and baby stuff, tears formed in the corners of his eyes. He looked perplexed. "This is incredible. Where did you say you found all of this?"

"I found the box in the garage after it fell off one of the top shelves, but look, there's something more," I said as I pointed to the pale pink envelope.

Hands shaking, he picked up the letter and stared at it. "I never wanted to open this because I never wanted Mom to leave us. She gave me that letter right before I took her to the hospital to give birth to you. Luci, please shut the TV off, and I'll read it out loud to both of us. Are you sure you feel up to this?"

I nodded and did as he instructed while he carefully opened the envelope. He read the first few lines and cried before he composed himself to read her letter aloud.

"Dear Kyle and my soon to be daughter Lucia,

"In the event of my death, I want you to know how much I love you. Kyle, I love you more than life itself. I know what a great Dad you'll be. I haven't met our beautiful daughter yet, but I already love her and hope to watch her grow up with all my heart.

"Because my love for you both is so deep, I want you to always be happy. This may be an uncomfortable topic for you on a day that will be filled with joy, but if anything should happen to me, I want you to live your life to the fullest. Kyle, I want you to find someone to love and have that love returned. For Lucia, I hope this new woman in her life will love and take care of her as if Lucia were her own daughter. Remember, you have my blessing. I hope you never have to open this letter, but if you do, please remember my words.

All my love now and forever,
Julie"

When he finished reading, we both sobbed. "Luci, your mom was an incredibly selfless woman to write a letter like this. I love her and miss her every day. She has always been my first and only love. That's why my feelings for Sage make me feel so guilty. I don't know what to do."

I remembered Mom's spirit said she wanted us to be happy and for Dad to find someone. "Dad, I'm sure Mom meant what she wrote in her letter. She wants us to be happy. You need someone to share your life, and I need a good friend, and Sage is that person."

Dad shook his head as he placed the letter back in its envelope and into his top shirt pocket. "I hurt Sage as badly as I thought I hurt your mother's memory. Sage must think I'm a selfish, uncaring man to treat her like that. I have to apologize, but will she even meet with me?"

I paused for a few minutes. "Maybe I should call Sage and start with something cheerful like asking if there's any more of that black and white cake left. If she says there is, I'll ask if we could come over so we could talk to her about what happened earlier." I paused. "Don't worry, Dad. I'm sure she'll say 'yes.' When you see Sage, you will apologize and tell her how you feel about her, how you felt when you left the cemetery, and about the letter we found. How does that sound?"

Dad shook his head. "Pretty darn wise coming from a thirteen year old and much better than anything I could come up with. I'm so lost at the moment. I'm not thinking straight."

"Ready?" I asked as I took my cell out of my shorts' pocket and called Sage. I hoped she would answer after seeing the call came from my cell number. She did but sounded puzzled.

"Luci, are you all right? I still don't understand what happened today. Your dad and I were so happy. Why would your dad break my heart like that?"

I responded in a caring tone. "Sage, I'd love to see you. There is no excuse for what he did, but today was a tough day for Dad, and I know he didn't handle it well. May Dad and I come over so he can explain and apologize?"

I heard her sob a very curt "no" before I asked, "By the way, any cake and ice cream left?"

Sage responded. "The entire cake is left, and I need someone to share it with me. Yes honey, please come over. You know how much I care about you and bring Chester. Your dad sure didn't handle today well at all. He broke my heart into little pieces. I don't care if I ever see him again so he can stay home." I heard more sobs break up her words.

"Sage, I care about you too. Please let him come. We found a letter from my mom that she had written on the day I was born, and he'd like to share it with you."

There was silence for a few seconds before she said. "I guess if you must, bring Kyle, but know that I would rather not see him or speak to him again. He can speak to me at my front door. I don't want him in my home." She added with a great deal of hurt in her voice.

"Thank you for that. We'll be there in about twenty minutes."

I hung up, smiled, and winked at Dad. "Please clean up and get ready to go to Sage's. We'll visit Lily, the florist, and you'll buy the biggest bouquet she has in the store. Like you always told me, you only get one chance at a do-over, so don't mess this one up."

Dad nodded. "Got it, Luci. You're the best daughter in the universe. I just hope Sage will understand how I felt and, after I read her the letter, will want to see me and give me a chance to apologize."

CHAPTER TWELVE

Dad, Chester, andI left Lily, the florist, for Sage's, carrying the biggest bouquet of multi-colored roses she had in the store. When we pulled into Sage's driveway, I saw her peek out her front living room window. She didn't come out right away to greet us, so I knocked on her front door, advising Dad to stand behind me. "Sage, Luci and Chester here, please come to the door. Dad has something important to say to you about this morning."

Sage opened the front door a crack. She saw Dad standing behind me, holding that enormous bunch of flowers and started to slam the door shut. Dad jumped in front of me and stopped the door from closing with his foot. He asked. "Sage, I want to apologize. May I come in so we can talk?"

Sage looked like she had been crying. "Whatever you have to say, you can tell me here."

Dad swallowed hard. "Sage, I don't know where to begin. First, I want to apologize to you for my shameful behavior this morning. As you know, Luci and I went to the cemetery for our yearly visit to Julia's grave, which always makes me cry, but this year, my sadness was accompanied by intense guilt. I felt guilty about falling in love with you, guilty for not wearing my wedding ring, and in a weird way, guilty because I was so happy for us while Julie was gone. That just didn't seem right to me."

Sage sighed and wiped tears from her eyes. "I went through similar feelings after Brandon died. I felt so guilty when I took off my engagement ring. I thought by not wearing the ring, I hurt him, but I only hurt myself by thinking that way. You know I never dated anyone else until I met you. You made me so happy and excited about the future.

"Trust me, I understand more than anyone how you felt this morning, but you didn't have to crush my love for you. You could have just explained your feelings without breaking up."

More tears streamed down Sage's cheeks. Dad took one of her hands while balancing the vase with the other. "If I may, I'd like to give you these roses as a token of my love. I'm so sorry about this morning. Sage, I want you to know my feelings for you have not changed."

Sage took the vase of roses from him as he continued. "If you'd let me, I'd like to read you a letter Luci found today in the garage. It dates back to the day Luci was born. I misplaced it and never opened it until this morning. It's personal and from my late wife. May we come in so I can share it with you?"

I interrupted, hoping to make them smile. "Besides, I'm starving and would like some of that cake and ice cream."

That brought smiles from Sage and Dad, so inside we went. Once we were all seated at her dining room table, Dad removed the letter from his pocket to read out loud to her. "I hope you'll give me another chance after hearing what Julie wrote to me the day she died."

When he finished reading, Sage wiped tears from her eyes, stood, and kissed Dad's cheek as she told him. "Kyle, I, more than anyone, can understand your feelings of guilt and sadness. I forgive your actions, but if you ever pull anything like this again, you, my love, will be history."

Dad stood and hugged her with the biggest smile on his face. "I don't want to leave you ever. I promise. I love you so much."

I clapped, and Chester howled with joy while C.C. pawed at his cage. We then celebrated with black and white cake and chocolate ice cream. Dad looked into Sage's eyes again. "I wanted to ask you before all this happened. I have something special planned for all of us on New Year's Eve. I wonder if you'd be my date."

Sage smiled. "I sure will."

~*~

New Year's Eve was only a few days away. Our small beach town held a big celebration each year because December 31st was the anniversary of our island becoming a town. There's a short parade, a bar-b-que on the beach with cupcakes, and at night fireworks over the Gulf. I wondered what Dad thought could be more special than that.

Dad, Chester, and I picked Sage up at five-thirty on New Year's Eve. She looked beautiful in a short red and white flowered sundress. We drove to the center of the island, where the party had already started. We parked in the designated lot to watch the parade before walking to the town beach for the barbecue and cupcakes. Dad had already bought our dinner tickets; the barbecue was delicious. We had our choice of hamburgers, hot dogs, chicken, and ribs. We filled our plates and added baked beans and cole slaw before we sat outside and shared one of the long metal tables set up for the event. Sage gushed. "This is so wonderful. I loved the parade with the school bands and all those colorful floats. The food is great, but I can't lie, dessert is always the best part of my meal. Those cupcakes are so pretty, and I can tell they are homemade!"

After we ate, we walked closer to the beach. A rock group entertained from the back of a large truck in the paved parking lot where we had parked. Dad strolled over to them and dropped money in their tip can. He waited for them to finish a song before he whispered something in the band leader's ear. I was puzzled at what it was.

Dad went back to our car and returned with three folding beach chairs and a blanket for Chester. He hoped to set them up to give us the best possible view of the fireworks. We then walked from the parking lot to the edge of the sand, where we all took off our shoes. A few minutes after Dad set our chairs in the sand, the leader of the rock group announced, "We have a special request for Sage." I looked over at her. Surprise was written all over her face.

The band played "I Love You Just the Way You Are." Dad smiled before he pulled Sage over to dance barefoot on the beach with him. It was dusk, and the moon began to rise in the sky over the water. Dad held Sage close before he spun her around on the sand a couple of times. He stopped dancing and got down on one knee. Everyone seated on their beach chairs near us cheered and clapped while Sage looked so stunned she placed her hands on her cheeks.

Chester barked as the clapping and cheering became louder. Dad reached into his shorts pocket to take out a small velvet box. He opened it to reveal an antique white gold ruby ring with diamonds as he cleared his throat. All of a sudden, the cheering stopped, and everyone around us became quiet.

Dad kissed Sage's hand and looked into her eyes. "Sage, I know we've only known each other a short time. But we're experienced enough in life to know not to let a good thing go. So when the right person comes along, you don't hesitate. You grab onto her and keep her close. I want to keep you close to me forever. Sage, will you marry me?"

Sage, teary-eyed, nodded and answered. "Yes, Kyle, I will. I love you and want to spend the rest of my life with you and Luci."

Dad took her left hand. "This ruby ring belonged to my great-grandmother. I want to give it to you as a symbol of our love." Dad then placed it on her left ring finger.

Everyone nearby began to clap and cheer louder than before. Chester wagged his tail like crazy, broke loose from my grip on his leash, and ran over to give the newly engaged couple some licks of his own. Of course, I got into the act with kisses and hugs as well.

Just then, as if on que, fireworks lit up the New Year's Eve sky. I looked up at all the colorful lights to see my favorite formations of bursting gold chrysanthemums, falling green willows, and pink peonies explode and leave trails of light as they fell from the sky. It was amazing and the perfect ending to a perfect day. The grand finale shot up more colorful patterns accompanied by all the oohs and aahs of the spectators.

I glanced at Dad and Sage. They paid no attention to the fireworks. Instead, they stared into each other's eyes as they kissed and held hands. The second the finale finished, a ring of small white sparkly lights sizzled in the night sky. They resembled the sparkly lights in my room that followed one of Mom's visits. Could these white lights be a sign from Mom? I looked up at the night sky and whispered, "Mom, I love you and miss you. You're always in my heart. Please send me a sign that you share our happiness."

Just as I finished those words, a woman with long blonde hair and wearing an old straw hat that covered part of her face seemed to come out of nowhere and walk in the moonlight through our small section of beach. She handed out small bags of different kinds of candy from a red, white, and blue basket for the town's birthday celebration. Each bag was a different color and contained different kinds of candy. The woman stopped next to me and handed me one but left before I could thank her.

When I opened my bag, I discovered it held chocolate kisses wrapped in silver foil. I smiled, content. Mom sent me a sign. I looked all over to find that woman, but she was gone, like she vanished into thin air. Stars twinkled in the sky just like those sparkling white lights after Mom's visit. Filled with love and all the happiness of the day, I grabbed Chester and gave him the biggest hug I could.

Dad's and Sage's happiness continued to be as electric as those colorful fireworks display that burst overhead on New Year's Eve. Never in my wildest dreams did I think a Wishing Cookie could bring a visit from Mom's spirit, make two people fall in love, and give me a loving friend I hoped to cherish for my entire life.

THE END

Mariah Lynne takes readers on breathtaking adventures. Whether traveling through time, solving a crime, or finding love in unlikely situations, her heroines are strong-willed, independent women whose memorable stories keep the pages turning.

A graduate of Syracuse University, Mariah, a New Jersey native, resides on a beautiful Florida Gulf Coast Island. Because she loves where she lives, Southwest Florida becomes the backdrop for all her stories. Before writing fiction, she owned and operated her own business and wrote weekly columns for two newspapers.

Mariah, an animal lover, always features a pet in every story.

In addition to A CHRISTMAS WISH FOR LOVE, her books include MAX CANINE CONCIERGE OF LOVE, PAWS FOR CHRISTMAS, THE DUCHESS' NECKLACE, SHADOWS ACROSS TIME, GEM OF A MURDER, CLAWS FOR JUSTICE, and THE LOVE GYPSY also available as an audiobook as well as other short stories.

When not writing, Mariah enjoys movies, swimming, and traveling with her husband.